Wanderlust

Frey

WANDERLUST

Jaimie L. Robertson

iUniverse, Inc.
New York Lincoln Shanghai

Wanderlust

All Rights Reserved © 2003 by Jaimie L. Robertson

No part of this book may be reproduced or transmitted in any form or by any means, graphic, electronic, or mechanical, including photocopying, recording, taping, or by any information storage retrieval system, without the written permission of the publisher.

iUniverse, Inc.

For information address:
iUniverse, Inc.
2021 Pine Lake Road, Suite 100
Lincoln, NE 68512
www.iuniverse.com

ISBN: 0-595-26887-0

Printed in the United States of America

This book is dedicated to Brianna, without whom I would never have had the courage to push myself forward and overcome obstacles.

I also dedicate this book to Kate Miotto and Trish Woo, who are not only the most talented and wonderful human beings I have ever had the pleasure to know, but who continually inspire me to delve into the world unknown and bring back those stories that must be told.

*Do you hear the siren's call
leading you into it all?
You follow all too willingly,
knowing not what you may see.*

*Behind every wandering heart
A spirit lies deep and dark.
Never take your eyes away
For your heart it will betray.*

❦   ❦   ❦

*Wandering halls
once laden with laughter,
he feels the encroaching chill.
It stalks him,
every now and then
licking at his heels with a cold tongue.
He pretends
it's all a dream
that he will soon wake from.
He still hears
the echo of voices
and sees phantoms of familiar faces.
He still feels
strong arms about him
whispering words he needs to hear.
Lost in thought,
he doesn't realize his peril
until the beast is upon him, the world fallen away.*

CHAPTER 1

❁

The night was strange. Not in any way that could be intuited by the senses, but in a way that was felt deep down in the soul. Above the clouds there was nothing to hinder the view of the moon and thousands of tiny stars. The world always seemed brighter and clearer at thirty thousand feet than it ever did on the ground. Yet tonight he felt on the brink of something.

As the plane began its descent, the ephemeral feeling slowly left him. Whatever uncanny quality about the sky above had given him a sense of the preternatural, it slowly dissipated as they moved down through the shroud of clouds and further still through a plain of fog. The change in air pressure caused his ears to pop, bringing him irrevocably out of his reverie.

Jonas Uhrig arrived at Richmond International airport on time. His flight from Cincinnati had been smooth, and he had been the only passenger in first class. He made his way down the ramp and out into the gate area. RIC was nearly deserted at this time of night. Only the soft hum of vending machines, the distant sound of a jet engine, and a few janitorial workers sweeping the floor with a soft swish broke the silence.

The distinct airport smell made him smile. He wasn't sure what elements made up that singular scent that was strictly reserved for airports and he didn't wish to. He knew only that it always made him feel at home. He moved quickly toward the baggage claim. He had no suitcase to retrieve. The small duffel slung over his shoulder contained everything he had needed for the trip. Rather, he was picking up his best friend.

Burke never liked to be kept waiting. If Jonas so much as stopped to check the local weather, Burke would greet him with that reproachful look he was so good at and would descend into a pout until Jonas made it up to him with a burger and a milkshake. Not that Jonas blamed him. He couldn't imagine that being locked up inside a cage in the noisy baggage compartment of a 737 would be much fun for anyone.

He pulled the claim papers from the inside pocket of his leather jacket and passed them over to the clerk. A skinny little man that Jonas judged to be somewhere between seventy and infinity who looked first at Jonas, then at the papers, and back to Jonas with an air of scrutiny a number of times. His pursed mouth pinched even more with every glance before he finally nodded and went to retrieve the kennel. Jonas wondered if dognapping was a serious problem or if the clerk was merely suspicious of everyone these days, as most airport personnel seemed to be. Not even the little old ladies of the world were safe from the critical eye of airport security anymore. He supposed it was inevitable, though regrettable.

The clerk returned with the kennel after what seemed an interminably long period of time. Jonas thanked the man, scooping up the kennel without even looking inside. He didn't need to. He heard the soft *chuff* from inside that meant Burke was going to insist on a burger and a milkshake whether or not Jonas had come directly to pick him up. Thankfully, Burke rarely barked. He was content with making his wishes known in a quiet mannerly way.

"It's almost midnight," Jonas said as he exited the airport and made his way to the long term parking garage. Tendrils of fog curled around him in the crisp autumn air. The yellow glow from the streetlamps added a sickly radiance to the mist.

Chuff.

"You'd think after all our traveling you'd be used to it by now."

GrrrCHUFF.

"You're a regular prima donna sometimes."

WhineChuff.

"Alright, alright," Jonas said. He set the kennel down beside the Maxima and unlocked the door. A rustling sound from inside the kennel told him that Burke was more than eager to get out of his confinement and into the soft leather seat. "A burger and milkshake it is. I could use some pure cholesterol myself."

He opened the passenger door and then unlocked the kennel. A flash of tan and sable fur flew past him as the border collie bounded into the passenger seat. Burke pricked up an ear and cocked his head, his back stiffening for an instant.

"What is it?" Jonas asked, briefly looking around. "Doggy jitters?"

Burke kept his pose a moment longer before relaxing, gazing up at Jonas with soulful eyes. Jonas shook his head and closed the door, putting the kennel and his duffel in the trunk before sliding behind the wheel. The dog was strange and often seemed afraid of some unseen danger, but on the whole he was a happy soul. Ever since turning up on his doorstep two years ago and refusing to leave, Jonas was constantly astounded by the dog's keen intelligence.

Jonas was greeted by Burke's grin as he started the engine. Despite his companion's aversion to airline travel, he loved to drive. Jonas often opted to drive instead of taking a plane to accommodate Burke, but sometimes the situation called for haste.

Through all this, Jonas never felt the presence that had followed him from the gate at the airport and out to his car. He had no precognition of danger, no prickling sensation at the back of his neck, no inexplicable need to look over his shoulder. He never saw the shadow that passed behind his car as he pulled out of the parking space and headed toward the I-64 onramp. To Jonas, there was only

Burke in the passenger seat, grinning and panting as they picked up speed.

❦ ❦ ❦

It took only minutes to reach the exit, and as he pulled into the drive thru of a late night fast food restaurant, Burke's panting picked up pace. He ordered two double cheeseburgers, one without bothersome vegetables and condiments in deference to Burke, two milkshakes, and an order of fries. The last were for Jonas. Burke still hadn't come to appreciate the fine flavor of crisped fried potato.

He put the large takeout bag on the floor of the passenger side, Burke looking longingly at the white gleaming paper as if it held the most valuable of treasures. Jonas figured that for a dog, a burger was indeed the most valued of treasures. He set the milkshakes in the two cup holders between the seats and pulled out onto the street. Burke settled back, but his eyes were still fixed on the bag.

"Not until we get home," Jonas said. Burke gave a half-hearted whine before sighing in defeat and looking out the window.

They rode in companionable silence the rest of the way, Jonas's mind on the trip now behind him, Burke's on the tantalizing smell of hamburger.

Jonas parked on the curb of the relatively quiet tree lined street in front of the large row house that he called home. It had been home since he was a small boy, and after the death of his parents fifteen years ago, he hadn't had the heart to sell it. Unlike those days however, he spent less than two months out of the year here. Coming back only between his endless trips, it was more of a way station than a home. However, he didn't believe in the sappy saying 'Home is where the heart is'. Home is where you keep your stuff, and this was the place he kept his.

Burke gently grabbed the bag off the floor, carrying it between his teeth. He was careful to lift it by the top, apparently not wanting to crush the precious contents. Jonas took the milkshakes, went around to get his duffel from the trunk, and then opened the door for Burke. As the dog exited the car and made his way across the cobblestone walk and up the steps, the front door opened.

"Right on time, as always," came the lilting Jamaican accent. "I don't suppose you'll be needin me to be makin any supper tonight."

"Not tonight, Bell," Jonas said, a smile breaking across his face as he took in the bright pink dress clinging to long ebony legs and crimson fingernails that his housekeeper was sporting. He wondered where she'd found the dress. It couldn't be easy finding such a garish wardrobe for someone who was six feet tall. "Nice getup. Got a date?"

"No," Belladonna's neon pink lips pursed into a pout. "It isn't easy for a lady to find the charmin company of another woman dese days. Dey're all so sexually repressed."

"You got that right," Jonas mumbled as he followed Burke into the foyer, setting his duffel on the floor. The scent of lemon oil and freshly cleaned rugs greeted him.

"What you talkin bout, pretty boy? Your only trouble wit women is gettin dem ta go away. Dey take one look at me and dey turn up deir pert little noses."

"It takes a special kind of woman to appreciate the kind of elegance and beauty you exude."

"A gentleman you are," Belladonna smiled and pinched his cheek affectionately. "But what you really meanin ta say is dat it takes a special kinda woman to love a cross-dressin former prostitute. Now go into da kitchen and feed dat dog before he pees da floor waitin for ya. I mean ta be outta here in two hours and no dog pee is keepin me from it."

Jonas gave her a wink and did as he was told. There wasn't any real fear of Burke peeing on the floor. The dog was meticulously neat and well-mannered, which suited Jonas perfectly. However, he knew that finding someone special was a sore spot with Bell lately, and he didn't want to make matters worse.

Jonas took the bag from the floor where Burke had placed it. The dog was sitting nearby in anticipation. Jonas unwrapped the burger and placed it in Burke's bowl and then poured the milkshake into the empty water bowl. "Have at it," he said.

Burke scrambled forward, chomping up the greasy fare with delight. Jonas unwrapped his own burger, but despite his earlier hunger, he found he no longer had the stomach for it. He grabbed a few French fries and sipped at his milkshake. He was suddenly very tired.

His latest series of wanderings had taken him to Toronto, Rome, Louisiana, Frankfurt, and finally Cincinnati. He hadn't been home in nearly six months. The constant need to travel, to *go* had started shortly after his parents had died in a plane crash off the coast of Florida. It began as a niggling sense of needing to be somewhere else, but over time had developed into a full blown obsession. He would wake in the middle of the night, sweating and gasping for air. Knowing he had to get out, had to *move*, had to find the source of his unrest. Sometimes he knew where he was going and sometimes he didn't know at all, just picked a city at random and went. He was sure any psychiatrist would have a field day with this frantic compulsive behavior.

When his Aunt Millie, seventy years old and his only living relative, had begun to question his odd behavior, he had told her he had taken a job as a freelance reporter. It had been a lie, but once the idea occurred to him, he decided it was just the thing to rid him of his boredom and to excuse his constant travel. Though Millie knew he didn't need the money, her brother having left him quite a sizeable inheritance, she approved of him doing something productive with his life. And though the meager income of a freelance reporter would do nothing to build the family's coffers, it was far better than him wasting his time gambling, partying, and womanizing as so many of his peers would have done if given the same set of circumstances.

Jonas had taken a few courses on journalism and then decided he would specialize in crime reporting. His father had owned a small publishing company that specialized in true crime novels, so it wasn't so far fetched that he would take an interest in that particular field. Besides, it seemed that everywhere he went these days, some heinous crime was occurring. He couldn't do anything to stop it, so he examined it, tore it down to its elements before building it back up from the foundation and reporting it. He could never quite make sense of the violence and tragedy that took place all around him in the world, but he could try.

He had been fairly successful in his career thus far. Newspapers thrived on crime and stories of the macabre and he was never short of papers wanting to publish his work. He had a talent for stumbling onto the best murder mysteries and real life tragedies. He also had a talent for writing them up in a tantalizing way that drew readers' attention like a train wreck. Editors invariably ate those stories up, never getting enough of it.

Jonas placed his own burger in Burke's bowl just as the dog finished his milkshake. "You need this more than I do," Jonas said, scratching him affectionately behind the ears. Burke licked his hand in pure canine love before turning his attention to the burger.

Jonas deposited the paper cups and wrappers in the trash can, a soft click and hum from the utility room telling him that Bell had started washing his clothes from the trip. He knew he could have gone the normal route to get a housekeeper who would also watch the property while he was away, one who was aware of proper etiquette and wasn't a cross-dressing former prostitute. However, at the time he had met Bell, she was just getting out of her life on the street. She had been the subject of an exposé he had done about the life of a prostitute, and over the three months he had done the story, he had come to like her a great deal. Not only for her strength and honesty, but the fact that twenty-two years on the streets hadn't hardened her beyond hope as it did so many.

Jonas had never thought of Belladonna as a he. Though she might have the standard equipment, she had the soul of a woman. Her preference for women over men simply meant she had the soul of a lesbian woman.

Jonas had needed a housekeeper. Belladonna had needed a job and a place to stay. It had worked out well, and though Belladonna had moved out last year, she still came to the house three times a week to check the mail, dust the place, and keep that lived-in feel. There was nothing worse than returning home to a dusty tomb-like house at the end of a long trip.

Jonas felt a cold nose against his hand and he reflexively began rubbing the smooth fur on the top of Burke's head.

"Ready for bed?"

Chuff.

"Come on, then. I'm beat."

Burke followed Jonas into the utility room as he said goodnight to Belladonna and then padded quietly upstairs to their room. The soft glow from the bedside lamp revealed that Belladonna had put clean linens on the bed, fluffed the pillows, and turned down the blankets. There were fresh towels in the bathroom, and the trio of candles on the dresser filled the air with a hint of jasmine. Burke stretched out on the floor, obviously enjoying the feeling of the plush carpet.

Jonas pulled on a fresh T-shirt and jogging pants. He never slept in anything he couldn't go out in public in. Sometimes the urge to leave gripped him out of the blue in the middle of the night and he couldn't waste the time to dress. He also kept a bag packed in the closet with everything he would need on a trip.

"Don't get too comfortable, bud. I don't think we're staying long this time," Jonas said.

Burke cocked his head to the side and rolled his eyes as if to say *Do we ever?*

"Smartass," Jonas muttered. He blew out the candles on the dresser and climbed between the sheets, sighing in pleasure at the feel of the soft fabric and surrounding warmth. He switched off the bedside lamp. In the distance, there was a rumble of thunder.

"'Night, bud."

Chuff.

❦   ❦   ❦

Reamun watched from his rental car as the lights went off upstairs inside the house. Uhrig wasn't what he had expected. He was less watchful, less aware of his surroundings, almost oblivious to the world around him. It was disappointing, but not something he would dwell on.

Ever since he had begun watching Jonas, he had felt that they had been lucky. He was healthy, strong, a formidable looking man with sharp intelligence and sound judgment. The fact that he showed no outward signs of change was troublesome, but also misleading. Reamun knew that since the death of his parents, Jonas had been experiencing a great deal of change within.

Reamun's plans called for a wealth of fortitude and cunning on Jonas's part, but he refused to believe that he had completely misjudged the man. It wasn't possible. Reamun would chalk it up to jet lag and fatigue. Soon Jonas would have to prove that he was much more than he seemed on the surface. Very soon.

Reamun switched on his phone, dialing a number from memory. After only one ring, a woman answered.

"It has begun," Reamun said.

"Are you there watching him?"

"Of course," said Reamun.

"Let me know how he does. I'm concerned…"

"You're always concerned. It's all going to work out perfectly."

"You don't know that," she said. "None of us can know that. It is up to Jonas and I don't believe he is ready yet," she said.

"He will be. I'll make certain of it."

CHAPTER 2

There was a preternatural quality about the night. Cincinnati was not known as a mecca of vampirism or the occult, nor did it possess anything she found even remotely intriguing. It wasn't the city that she found so unearthly. It was the night itself. She couldn't put her finger on the exact reason, but she felt it all around her. Though it could have been the corpse lying only fifty feet away, she didn't think that entirely explained the feeling of strangeness that saturated the night, making the chilly air seem oppressive as it swirled around her in slow serpentine motions. She had seen her share of corpses and crime scenes and none of them had given her this same skin-crawling sensation that swept over her now. Perhaps it was her fatigue, an overdose of caffeine from the four lattes she had in the past two and a half hours, or both.

Kate Barnett stood behind the yellow line of police tape and snapped several pictures of the crime scene. Murders were not her favorite jobs, but they paid the bills and ensured that she would have enough money to keep up her travels without fear of going hungry or getting stuck somewhere along the road with no money for gas.

This particular murder was a gruesome one. The sixty-eight year old proprietor of a small corner grocery had been taking out the day's garbage to the dumpster behind the store when he had been viciously attacked. He had been stabbed several times and his eyes neatly cut out of his head and left lying next to him on the pavement.

Though the back door to the grocery had been left unlocked, there had been nothing taken from the store. Even the cash register had been left untouched.

As she continued to snap pictures, ignoring the buzz of reporters and camera crews around her, she hoped that at least a few of them would turn out without the enormous backside of the detective who kept crossing her line of vision blocking the view of the scene. It seemed that every crime scene had at least one cop with a big ass that stood to block the views of onlookers. She wondered if it was procedure. Did they just take an already employed cop with a suitably large rump and plant him there? Or did they hire them for their well endowed behinds? Whatever the case, it was highly annoying.

When she saw one of the men reach for something on the ground and lift it up with one gloved hand, she shifted her focus to him, snapping off a series of pictures. She let her mind drift as she did so. She didn't want to think about the death and pain and fear that had taken place here. If she let herself get caught up in the moment, she'd be in a funk for days. This was just a job to pay the bills. She wasn't going to let herself become emotionally invested in it. Right.

She was an optimistic and outgoing person. It had been more of a survival trait in her youth. She had been raised by her mother who always insisted they stay on the move, never living in one city for more than a few years. Elaine Barnett was not a timid woman by any stretch of the imagination. Yet she always seemed to be looking over her shoulder. Her mother had never said so, but Kate had always known that they were hiding from her father, a man Elaine never spoke of and Kate never asked about. She had been afraid to ask.

After taking another roll of film, she packed away her gear and headed back to the Bronco. Her true passion was in nature photography, but the income from that work, when there was one, was slow in coming. The money didn't really matter much to her. She needed only enough for food, drink, clothing, camping gear, gas, and the occasional hotel room. She had no residence. Instead, she roamed the country and slept most nights beneath the stars, weather permitting.

Sometimes she longed for a home. A place to put down roots and build a cozy life in. Yet she didn't feel ready for that sort of responsibility. At twenty-nine, she was still trying to find her niche in the world. She had no idea where she wanted to live, much less any details on what sort of dwelling she wanted, what sort of curtains to buy, or whether or not she wanted a dog or a cat to complete the cozy little life that waited out there somewhere. These were all things she thought she would eventually figure out some day. As with many things, she was putting off *some day* for as long as she could.

In the parking lot across the street from the corner grocery, she climbed into the Bronco and headed for the newspaper offices where she would develop the latest round of pictures in time for the morning paper. She likely wouldn't finish until near dawn, but she didn't mind. She was a nocturnal creature by nature, and often found it easier to fall asleep as the sun rose than to waste away the quiet hours when everyone else was asleep. She preferred to work alone, and she also preferred driving the long distances between jobs in the dark hours of night when few other people were on the road.

It wasn't that she didn't like other people. She simply had trouble relating to them. So many people walked through life seeing nothing other than their insulated worlds and the perils and pitfalls of their everyday lives. They had lost the wonder and amazement that was all around them, had become desensitized to the very beauty of life.

As she pulled into the lot of the newspaper offices, she suddenly wished there were more people around. She normally enjoyed the stillness of night, but right now the night seemed not just still, but crouched like a lion in the shadows, awaiting the perfect opportunity to strike.

She climbed out of the Bronco and hurried inside, not wanting to be out in the deserted parking lot any longer than was necessary. She knew she wouldn't be sleeping outside tonight. She would have to spend the money for a hotel room.

While she worked in the dark room developing her pictures, she tried to figure out what it was that was making her so jittery. It had started when she got to the scene this evening.

Perhaps it was the murder, despite her carefully constructed wall to keep just those sorts of things from getting to her. It must have been the eyes. That wasn't something that was run-of-the-mill for her. People were often shot, stabbed, run over by buses, mauled by vicious dogs, but rarely did you see the sort of diabolical mutilation that left you cringing in horror.

How had the murderer been able to pull it off without anyone witnessing it? If he killed the victim first, that would have explained why no one heard anything. If the entire crime had taken place outside the store in the alley, how had the killer had time to remove the eyeballs and keep them intact?

The killer was either confident that he wouldn't be seen or simply reckless. She couldn't imagine the reckless personality went with the kind of psychosis that led one to cut out eyeballs from their sockets. Perhaps it was that very purposeful mutilation, the sort of person it would take to be able to do such a thing to another human being, which had her so shaken.

When she looked up at the pictures she had already done, the scrap of red fabric that one of the officers held caught her eye. She grabbed a magnifying glass from the counter to take a closer look. Her hands were shaking as she raised it to the picture. She already knew what she would find.

CHAPTER 3

Jonas woke suddenly, his heart pounding. He fumbled for the switch on the bedside lamp and squinted his eyes as light flooded the room. He looked about for the source of his unease and saw that Burke was standing at the bedroom door, his back tense, ears flattened against his head, a soft growl issuing from deep inside his throat.

Jonas sat up and pressed a hand to his temple, trying to clear his head. "What is it, bud?"

Burke glanced at Jonas, whined, pawed at the door, and resumed his alert stance. Jonas looked at the clock. Two fifteen. He had been asleep less than an hour and a half. He threw back the covers and climbed out of bed. He approached the door, listening for any sounds. He heard nothing.

"You smell a cat?"

Burke growled, his eyes still intent upon the door. Jonas had never seen him so upset before. A cold chill raced up his spine.

"Alright, let's have a look."

As soon as he opened the bedroom door, Burke was out and down the steps in a flash. Jonas tried to call him back, afraid that an intruder would harm the dog, but Burke was having none of it. Jonas followed more cautiously, alert for any noises. When he reached the foot of the stairs, he found Burke standing at the entry door. He barked once, a low threatening sound that Jonas had never before heard him make.

"What is it?" Jonas asked, peering out the front window. The street was deserted. The chilly November night seemed suspended in time. The trees were absolutely still. Burke growled low and pawed the door. Jonas hesitated. If this were just a cat, Jonas was going to be hopping mad. On the other hand, if it were some real threat, he was ill prepared to handle it.

Burke barked again, more insistently.

"Alright," Jonas conceded. He hurried upstairs and slipped on his tennis shoes, grabbing his cell phone from the dresser. He had no weapon to take with him and wasn't sure he would take it if he did have one. He had always abhorred violence. He saw far too much of it in his line of work. He had tried to understand what drove people to it, but other than defending oneself or a loved one in a life threatening situation, he couldn't fathom what it was that brought people to physically hurt one another. If he had a weapon, he would most likely delay so long in using it that either it would be useless or the attacker would use it against him.

He headed back down to the foyer and slipped on his jacket. He punched in the numbers nine-one-one on his phone so all he would have to do is hit the send button if indeed this were an actual emergency and not just a show of canine insanity.

Jonas clipped the leash to Burke's collar, not wanting to risk the dog's safety in light of his obvious distress. He took one last look out the window, hoping to get some idea of what was going on. Burke pulled at the leash and barked again. Jonas knew there was nothing to do but go out there.

When he opened the door, Burke rushed forward, dragging Jonas along as he scrambled down the steps. The dog turned north on the cobblestone walkway, pulling forcefully at the leash in his haste.

Jonas held tight, all his senses alert as Burke dove out into the night in front of him. The night was still, shrouded in mists. The glow of the streetlamps did very little to chase away the gloom, seeming only to serve as faraway beacons in the night. Jonas could almost imagine that he and Burke were the only living things for many miles.

As they neared the short alleyway that connected this row of houses with the ones to the west, Burke slowed, growling low in his throat as he moved. Jonas's free hand went to the cell phone in his pocket, his finger on the send button.

From the alleyway he heard a muffled curse, sounds of a struggle, and then a shrill pain filled scream split through the night air. He pushed the send button on the phone, his grip loosening a fraction on the leash in his panic. Burke chose that instant to tug hard against his leash once more, freeing himself from Jonas's grip.

"Shit," Jonas muttered, racing after the dog. There was no doubt about now, something far worse than a cat was lurking in the night. Unless it was a really big cat who could curse effectively.

Burke was barking wildly now, racing around the corner and out of sight. "Shit," Jonas muttered again, following close behind. He wasn't sure what he would find around that corner, but Burke's safety overrode his own sense of self preservation. Burke was more than just a dog or a companion. He was family. Most of the time he was the only thing that kept Jonas out of perpetual gloom.

Jonas rounded the corner, taking in the scene quickly. A dark figure raced away and into the adjoining street to the west, another figure lay sprawled on the cobblestone, face down and unmoving. Burke was chasing after the retreating figure.

"Burke, stop! Are you crazy?!" Jonas was about to follow when Burke stopped at the end of the alley, staring south down the street to where the attacker had fled. Jonas let out a sigh of relief. "Come here, boy."

Burke looked down the street and then back at Jonas, finally electing to stay with Jonas. He padded back to the still figure on the ground. Jonas followed. It wasn't until he was nearly on top of the victim that he saw the bright pink dress now spattered in blood. The once brightly glowing neon lips were now split and bleeding. The side of her head was battered, making her almost unrecognizable.

Burke whined, nuzzling her shoulder.

"Shit," Jonas said once more and finally remembered the cell phone in his pocket.

🍁   🍁   🍁

"Let's go over this again," said Detective Hernandez, flipping through his legal pad before leveling a suspicious stare at Jonas.

"Let's not and just say we did," Jonas said, rubbing Burke's head. "We've been over it a dozen times now. If I think of anything more, I'll be sure to give you a call. I need to get to the hospital to check on Bell and see if she's going to make it."

"You think he won't live?" Hernandez asked, leaning forward. Through the entire hour and a half that Jonas had been stuck with the detective in his living room, the man had made a point of referring to Belladonna as a he and not-so-subtly inferring that he suspected Belladonna and Jonas were more than just friends. Jonas knew this was some sort of ploy to get his dander up, but it wasn't working. Technically, Bell was a he, but anyone who knew her would never associate her with the male gender. And anyone who knew either of them very well knew that the chances of them sleeping together were less than that of being struck by lightning.

"Did you see her? Her head was bashed in, she was stabbed several times, and half her face was gone," Jonas said, leaning forward himself. "I have no idea what the extent of her injuries are, but she didn't look like she'd be dancing a jig anytime soon. I've seen enough victims of this sort of crime in my line of work to know her chances aren't good. Now if you'll excuse me detective, I'll be on my way. If you think of any original questions, you can call me." Jonas fished a business card out of his pocket and passed it to the surly detective.

"It is in your best interests to cooperate with us, Mr. Uhrig."

"And I've done that. Now it is in my best interests to see how my friend is doing." Jonas stood, and Burke did the same.

Hernandez said nothing, merely scowled as he stood and met Jonas at the door. Jonas held it open as Hernandez left, barely repressing the urge to call the detective on his asinine behavior.

❋ ❋ ❋

When Jonas stepped outside he saw that the street was now empty. A blanket of silence lay over the city in darkness. The TV news vans had gone, the forensics team had tagged and bagged what little they could find, and the officers had questioned the neighbors. They were either really quick or they didn't really give a damn one way or the other. Jonas suspected the latter was most likely the case.

If it had been some pretty young college girl from a good family, there was no doubt in his mind that the investigation would have been more thorough. The only reason they had bothered at all was because by morning, they would likely have a murder case on their hands instead of an assault. An unsolved murder was never good for anyone's political career.

Virginia had been a leader in murders per capita for several years before the politicians had finally made it a campaign issue. What they came up with was Project Exile. A tough series of laws aimed at ridding the streets of criminals with guns. In theory, it sounded perfect and the numbers seemed to back that up. However, Jonas wasn't always sure they were worried about getting the right guy as long as someone was put away for the crime and their statistics were tidied up.

Virginia now led the country in executions per capita in states with over one million residents and was second only to Texas in total number of executions. Very few death sentences were ever overturned on appeal. Jonas often wondered how many of those executed each year were actually guilty.

"C'mon, Burke. Let's see if they missed anything."

Chuff.

Jonas pulled a small penlight out of his jacket pocket as they entered the alley. It wasn't much of a light source, but he wasn't expecting to find anything. He knew he was procrastinating. He knew that when he got to the hospital he would be faced with either Bell's corpse or a vegetable. Either way he wasn't sure he could handle it.

He moved the penlight over the cobblestones, trying not to concentrate on the blood soaked ground. If he looked too long, his mind would start calculating the amount of blood loss, the force of the impact of Bell's head against the brick wall, the angle the knife must have stabbed her from. Those were things he could think about later. Right now he was just fighting exhaustion and the need to throw up.

Woof.

Jonas looked up at the soft but insistent noise from Burke. He was staring into the shadows at the end of the alley, sniffing the air.

"What is it, bud?"

Whine.

Jonas moved to Burke's side, crouching down to run a calming hand over his back. He shone the penlight into the shadows and saw a scrap of gossamer crimson fabric pressed against the building. A chill of recognition crawled up his spine. He dug around in his jacket pocket and produced a pencil. A journalist's best friend. He lifted the fabric, and saw that it was a scarf. He turned it in the light knowing what he would find, but not knowing *how* he knew. One black eye staring back at him. The eye of Horus. It was an Egyptian symbol, but he could not immediately recall its significance or meaning.

Whine.

Jonas put the penlight back in his pocket and scratched Burke behind the ears. "Let's go back to the house. We've got work to do."

Reamun sat across from the alley and watched as Uhrig and the dog found the scarf. Good. His instincts were better than they had first appeared to be. The real test would be what Uhrig decided to do with the scarf. Reamun let out a sigh of anticipation. The next phase was about to begin.

He watched as Jonas picked up the scarf with the tip of a pencil. He didn't reach for his cell phone. Didn't fish around for the detective's card.

"Good boy," Reamun said. He wondered if Jonas felt the familiarity of the cloth, if he recognized the design embroidered in the center. He could almost taste the other man's fear. "What are you thinking?"

He smiled as Jonas stood and began walking back to the house, not once reaching into his pocket for the phone.

Jonas laid the scarf on his desk and opened his laptop. He pressed the power button and went downstairs and into the kitchen to make coffee. Burke followed him with curiosity, watching as he paced the floor while waiting for the coffee to brew.

"I've seen it somewhere," Jonas said. "The scarf. It means something."

Burke said nothing, merely watched as Jonas continued pacing and talking.

"Was it Phoenix? No. Maybe it was one of the California killings. Could be Vancouver. Damn. Could be anywhere." Jonas ran a hand through his dark hair. He hadn't combed it since going to bed, nor had he ever changed out of his jogging pants and T-shirt.

"Somewhere. One of the cases. It was just in the past year or so I think. Not this last round of trips. Before. Something about a red scarf...something..."

Jonas paced to the pantry to get the dry dog food. He noted that Belladonna had cleaned both bowls before leaving. Before she had been brutally assaulted in an alleyway. He could imagine the terror she must have felt. He shook his head and poured the dog food. He filled the water bowl and then paced some more, trying to remember where he had seen the scarf before and how he had known the Eye of Horus would be on it.

Burke made no move to go eat. His eyes followed Jonas as he pulled a coffee mug out of the cabinet, dumped the filter from the coffee machine into the trash, rinsed the basket and placed it back on the machine. Jonas poured coffee into the mug, spilling some over his hand in his preoccupation with his thoughts, cursed, went back to the sink to run his hand under the water, grabbed some paper towels, cleaned up the spill, put the paper towels into the trash, and finally picked up the mug and headed upstairs to his study.

Burke padded quietly after Jonas as he sat down at his desk, setting the coffee aside. Burke curled up on the floor at his feet. Jonas first looked through his files, hoping that just the names of the articles he had written would spark his memory. It didn't work. He opened up Explorer, clicked on search and entered the words "red" and "scarf", telling the program to search only within the text of the files in the directory in which he kept his articles.

After a moment the computer returned three results. The first was an article he had written eight months ago on a gruesome slaying of a thirteen year old girl in Philadelphia which was still unsolved. He clicked on the file, and skimmed through it, the details of the case rushing back in a flood through his mind.

The girl had been on her way home from a friend's house only two blocks from where she lived. It was just after dark when she had called her mother to say she was coming home. The girl never made it. Thirty minutes later, her father had walked down the street to see what was keeping her. He found several people in the street. Some screaming, some crying, one man talking excitedly into a cordless phone. At first he had thought young Jenny had been hit by a car, but once he saw her body, it was clear something much more gruesome had occurred. She had been stabbed over twenty times, and her throat slashed so deeply that it had nearly severed her head.

None of the neighbors had heard anything. No one saw anything. The only evidence left at the scene was a single red scarf found beneath the body when the coroner had moved it. Though they had used every resource possible, the police had never turned up a suspect. No leads, no other clues, no hope of finding the killer.

Jonas looked for any mention of an insignia on the scarf, but there was no mention of one. This meant that either the police hadn't disclosed the information or there hadn't been one. Jonas connected the printer cable to the laptop and printed off a copy of the article. Then he closed the file and brought up the next article.

This one was a beating in Santa Monica from when he had visited two years ago. It had been a young man this time. Twenty-two year old Lance Morgan had been accosted on his way home from a bar. He had been beaten with a blunt object and left for dead behind a dumpster. A red scarf was found lying on top of his leather jacket when he was found by the driver of the disposal service truck the next morning. Morgan had survived, though he would be confined to a wheelchair for the rest of his life. Upon waking, Morgan had no memory of the incident, or the entire week leading up to it. It had been deemed a random attack by police and the case was never solved. No mention of a design on the scarf.

Jonas printed this article as well and then pulled up the last one. This one was a murder in Vancouver five years ago. Forty-six year old Bethany Williams had been found in her garage, bludgeoned to death with a wrench. A red scarf was found at the scene by police with what they described as an Egyptian design on it. In his follow-up article, he found that they had convicted her ex-husband of the murder and he was now serving a twenty-five year sentence. No further mention was made of the scarf.

How had he known the design would be the Eye of Horus? Maybe it had been a wild guess, his brain remembering the fragment about Egyptian symbolism, but it seemed so obscure to him. He had known not only that it was the Eye of Horus, but that it would be embroidered in delicate black thread, centered on the flimsy fabric, staring at him. He had seen it in his mind before he ever picked up the scarf with the pencil.

"How could I know that?"

Burke lifted his head from the floor, but made no sound. Jonas reached out a hand to rub his head. After a moment, Burke rested his head back on his paws and closed his eyes.

"Maybe I just didn't put it in the article. Maybe they told me, but I just didn't put it in there." Jonas sighed. "No. If I had known, I would have put something like that in the article. It's too damn weird not to add. I remembered every detail of those cases. All of them. Except for the scarf. Why?"

Jonas's phone rang and he pulled the phone out of his pocket and answered. "Uhrig."

"Jonas, what the hell happened? I just watched the morning news."

Jonas was relieved to hear Raiden's voice. The two of them had been friends since journalism school and found they had a great deal in common. They were about the same age, both were over six feet tall, and both had dark coloring. Raiden also loved to travel. Though he didn't have a compulsion as Jonas did, he was a free spirit and roamed wherever his mood took him.

He tended to indulge himself much more than Jonas. He went through women like most people went through underwear. He liked to drink and party and generally have a good time. Jonas was much more serious-minded, but they always enjoyed each other's company and tended to understand each other's quirks.

They didn't see each other much over the years, but kept in touch by email and phone. Whenever they were in the same town at the same time, they shared a few beers and caught up. To Jonas, the relationship seemed more like brothers than friends. Neither he nor Raiden had immediate family to rely on, so in those times when they would normally go to family, they relied on each other.

"Bad night," Jonas said.

"Sounds like it. Bell?"

"Don't know yet. I'm getting ready to leave for the hospital soon."

"I can meet you there," he said. "I'd like to see how she is myself."

Jonas knew Raiden was more interested in how he was doing than Belladonna. It was his way of assuring himself that Jonas was okay and didn't require a night of drunken forgetfulness or some other device that Raiden often used in times of trouble. "Good. I'll meet you there in an hour."

"I'll be there," Raiden said.

As he hung up, those three words still echoed in his mind. I'll be there. Somehow a sense of rightness came back to the day with those three words. Raiden would be there. Everything would be alright.

Jonas decided to call in a favor from another friend. He dialed a number and it was answered on the second ring.

"Yeah?" the voice on the other end of the line sounded bored.

"Rob, it's Jonas. I need to call in that favor."

"Sweet Jesus," Rob Woo said. "Please tell me this will be relatively painless."

"A lot less painful than getting booted from MIT would be," Jonas said. "And relatively simple compared to the leg work I did to get those hacking charges dropped. How's your father?"

"Doing well. Business is good. Apparently no lack of crime to keep the publishing business going. It's been fifteen years since you sold him your Dad's publishing company and it gets busier every day. Maybe good for us, but not so good for the rest of the world. What's the favor?"

"I need you to do some checking. It's got to be thorough and it's got to be kept quiet. At least for right now. Can you handle it?"

"Sounds serious," Rob said, keen interest creeping into his voice. "I'm in."

"I need you to look for any violent assaults or killings over the last ten years where a red scarf was found at the scene."

"What area?"

"All of them," Jonas said. "I've found three so far. Philadelphia, Santa Monica, and Vancouver over the last five years."

"And you think they're connected?"

"Could be. I don't know. I just know that there was a red scarf found at the scene of all three crimes within inches of the bodies. Can you do it?"

"Yeah," Rob said. "It'll take me a day or two to get back to you. What's this about?"

"Bell was assaulted last night. I found a red scarf at the scene and it reminded me of something. I did some digging and came up with those other three, and those were just the ones I'd covered. There could be more."

"Damn, is she okay?"

"Don't know," Jonas said. "Doesn't look good."

"Alright. Just gimme a day or two to get it done and I'll email you the results."

"Thanks."

Jonas switched off the phone, stood and stretched. He knew that if the information was out there, Rob would find it. He looked at the monitor, checking the time on the taskbar. Six forty-eight. It was going to be a very long day. "No rest for the weary."

Burke raised an eyebrow, but didn't lift his head from the floor.

Jonas went into his room. The scent of jasmine still clung to the air. He glanced longingly at his bed and then turned instead to the bathroom. He would take a hot shower and then go to the hospital, he thought. As long as he found no other convenient excuses to delay him.

CHAPTER 4

She was going to live. Jonas stood staring down at the still form on the bed, wanting to reach out a hand to touch her smooth ebony skin to assure himself it was still warm. He found it difficult to believe that the severely distorted and swollen figure lying in the bed was his friend.

The doctors had no idea what condition she would be in when she woke. The extent of the head injuries was serious, but only time would tell they said. A full recovery was possible. It was also possible that she would be mentally damaged beyond the ability to function.

Jonas looked down at the long crimson nails lying against the stark white linen. Some of them had broken or torn in her struggle. For the first time in a long while, he felt completely insignificant. He had no power over the inevitable tide of human suffering that eventually washed over everyone, even those he loved. All he could do was stand by and watch the pain.

Not for the first time, he wondered if his endless wanderings were spurred by the hope that he could outrun that tide. Perhaps if he kept moving, never allowing himself to stay in one place, the tide would pass him by. It was a ludicrous notion of course, but Jonas could think of no other reason for it. It was more than an impulse control issue. It was a need, a calling, something he was incapable of refusing.

He had tried in the past to ignore it, but had never been successful. If he didn't go when the feeling of need overcame him, he began to get sick. He would shake, vomit, become incapable of clear thought. Eventually he would pass out from pain and fatigue and when he woke, he would be on his way to some far away destination.

A nurse shuffled in, a solemn expression pasted on her face. It was the same expression he had seen on everyone's face in the ICU. He supposed it came with the territory.

"Kicking me out?"

"Afraid so."

"If I leave a card, can someone call me if she wakes up? I'm not sure I'll be able to make it back soon."

"Sure. As long as the cops don't have a problem with it. Leave your number with the desk nurse."

Jonas thanked her and left his card with the ICU desk and met Raiden in the waiting room. The hospital only allowed one visitor per patient on the ICU floor, and Raiden had been content to wait.

"How is she?" Raiden asked as he put down the magazine that he had only been half-reading.

"Going to make it," Jonas said. "But she looks terrible."

"She'd smack you if you said that to her face," Raiden smiled.

"She'd probably knock me on my ass," Jonas agreed.

"Any idea who did this?"

"No," Jonas said. "It would seem to be a random act of violence."

"Is that what the cops think?"

"Unless they think it was me," Jonas said.

"You? Now that's a laugh. I'm surprised you can walk down the street without fearing you'll inadvertently squish a bug."

"My sympathies don't extend to insects. I try not to squish spiders though."

"Tough break for the bugs. That's discrimination."

"Good thing the law doesn't extend to bugs then," Jonas said.

"Want to grab some lunch?"

"Not hungry. Besides, I need to go by the library and then get back to the house. Burke needs to be fed."

"Alright then. Tell fur face I said hi. I've got plans tonight, but I can ditch them. Just let me know if you need anything. Anything at all, Jonas," Raiden said, laying a hand on Jonas's shoulder.

Jonas smiled. "I will. Thanks."

He headed out to his car. He had felt uneasy leaving Burke at home alone, but he would have felt no better leaving him in the car. At least one of them had gotten some sleep.

As Jonas got into the car and pulled out of the parking garage, he went over the events of the previous night in his mind. The entire thing still felt surreal, but it also felt familiar. As if he should have somehow expected it, should have known it was going to happen. As if he should somehow know what would happen next.

"You're losing it, Uhrig," Jonas said aloud. "Next thing you know, you'll be talking to yourself."

※ ※ ※

Reamun followed the Maxima at a discreet distance. So far he wasn't disappointed in his subject. The fact that Uhrig hadn't yet sensed him following simply meant that he was doing a good job of staying hidden. The man had no reason to believe he was being tailed, no inkling that life as he knew it was changing forever, no idea that he was just now starting down a path that would bring all his beliefs crashing down around him.

The man would have to hone his skills and quickly, but Reamun had no doubts that Jonas Uhrig possessed the key elements that would be needed. Why else would the dog have sought him out and stayed with him so long? The dog might have to be dealt with, of course.

Reamun knew that it wouldn't prove an easy task, but he wasn't going to let that thought enter his mind. He was focused. He would not let anything go wrong. It was all under control. Just as he liked it.

❦   ❦   ❦

Jonas had spent nearly an hour at the library looking through old articles and then on information regarding the Eye of Horus. He'd had a bit of luck, but not enough. He pulled up in front of the house, parking at the curb. He expected to see Burke at the window, but there was no sign of the dog. Jonas hoped he was taking a nap. For a dog, the animal slept very little. He always seemed to be looking out the windows or just pacing the room. He had taken Burke to the vet last year to find out the cause of his insomnia, and the vet had given him some mild tranquilizers to help Burke sleep. Burke had refused to take them, and had been uncharacteristically distraught when Jonas had tried to slip them in his food.

Jonas had given up then, feeling guilty at trying to trick Burke into taking the medicine. If he wanted to stay up, he'd let the mutt stay up. He didn't seem to be suffering any malaise or infirmity from his lack of sleep, but Jonas still worried from time to time.

Jonas turned the key in the deadbolt and realized the door wasn't locked. His heart skipped a beat. He had locked the door. He remembered it clearly. The only other people who had a key were Belladonna and his Aunt Millie. Belladonna was unconscious at the hospital and Millie was in Georgia.

It dawned on him then that Belladonna hadn't had her purse when he'd found her. If the attacker had taken her purse, he had also taken the keys to Jonas's house which were inside. Suddenly he was gripped with terror. Burke.

Jonas pushed open the door, stepping inside as quietly as possible. The living room was a wreck. All the furniture had been upended and torn, the paintings and photographs lying smashed and broken on the floor. Lamps shattered. No Burke.

He thought for a moment about using the cell phone in his pocket to call the police, but quickly rejected the idea. If the beeps from dialing the phone didn't alert the intruder, his talking would. He wasn't about to leave the house long enough to make the call when Burke was somewhere inside and in all likelihood wounded or in danger.

Jonas checked the coat closet. Boxes littered the floor, coats torn apart at the seams, scraps of paper everywhere. No Burke. He moved through the foyer and into the living room. He decided to check out the kitchen and dining room before moving upstairs. He didn't want to risk leaving the intruder down here hiding somewhere.

More debris littered the dining area. The crystal chandelier which had been his mother's pride and joy now lay in a thousand tiny pieces scattered about the room. He didn't care. He would worry about the destruction of irreplaceable objects later. He had to find Burke.

He moved across the dining room, attempting to make his way through without stepping on the tiny crystal shards. He couldn't afford to make any noise. As he passed through the archway leading into the kitchen, he heard a muffled *thump* from upstairs. Burke? Or the intruder?

He scanned the kitchen, bath, and utility room only briefly as he made his way to the steps and ascended them, staying close to the left wall as he had learned to as a small child when he was sneaking downstairs for a snack.

It occurred to him just how completely insane his life had become since the death of his parents. He wondered if he were responsible for all of it somehow. Had his own discontent and unhappiness led to all this?

Just below the upstairs landing, he found a pool of blood soaking steadily into the runner and dripping down the polished mahogany stairs. *Please*, he thought. *Don't let it be Burke's.*

Jonas paused a moment, listening to the house. It seemed to him to be completely devoid of sound, as if he had been suddenly struck deaf. He waited a moment longer, and then he moved silently to the study door and eased it open.

Everything was destroyed except for his laptop, which was nowhere in sight. He checked the closet and found that most of his files were missing as well. *What the hell is going on?*

He left the door to the study open and moved across the hall to the spare bedroom. The door was slightly ajar, and he pushed it back slowly. Here the destruction was less overwhelming. A lamp shattered, the mirror on the vanity broken, the linens torn from the bed, but nothing serious. He checked under the bed. No Burke. He checked in the closet. No Burke. He made a quick check of the hall bath. No Burke.

None of the expensive paintings or electronics other than his laptop seemed to be missing. The extent of the destruction wasn't what you would expect to find in the search for valuables. It was done out of anger or hatred. Destruction for the sake of destruction.

Moving to his bedroom door, he mentally steeled himself for what he would find. Whatever was beyond, he could handle it. Unless Burke was dead. *Don't think about it.*

He opened the door quickly, without any heed for the noise he made. Blood. So much blood. He gripped the door frame as he looked around at the total devastation before him. He moved around the bed, stepping over debris, attempting not to step in the gore. No Burke. He looked in the closet. No Burke. He looked in the bathroom. No Burke. From above him, he heard another thump. *The attic.*

Moving as quickly as possible. He went back to the closet and looked up at the hatch that led to the attic. It was open, and one large bloody handprint showed where the intruder had lifted himself up into the opening. Jonas jumped, grabbing the edge, swinging himself up with ease. He braced his weight on his arms as he swung his legs up. Shafts of light shone in like beams of gold through the darkness. The vent on the far side had been torn away from its fastenings.

"Burke?" Jonas called.

A quiet *chuff* from the other end of the attic had him nearly collapsing with relief. Jonas scrambled to the other side across the two by fours, trying to hurry, but also not wanting to take a wrong step and plunge through the ceiling.

He found Burke sitting by the opening left by the vent. His face and paws were covered in blood.

"Shit," Jonas said.

Chuff. Burke looked at him seriously, as if to say he agreed with Jonas's assessment of the situation.

It took a moment of looking the dog over to realize that he didn't appear to be wounded. Jonas looked out onto the rooftop. Whoever the intruder had been, he had gone now. And he had at least one very nasty dog bite.

"So, you're Rambo dog now?" Jonas asked, his voice shaking with a mixture of relief and the aftermath of his adrenaline rush.

Burke grinned at him.

"C'mon. We have to call the cops."

Burke followed, walking across the boards with ease. It wasn't until Jonas reached the opening to the closet below that he wondered how in the hell Burke had gotten up here. He looked at the dog. Burke's eyes were wide and full of doggy innocence.

"This is insane," Jonas said.

Burke grinned.

🍁   🍁   🍁

"Looks like you're having a run of bad luck," Detective Hernandez said, eyeing the destruction in the living room.

"It appears that way. So if you don't mind, let's cut the bullshit. I'm not in the mood."

"Fine by me. Who hates you?"

"No one that I'm aware of."

"Really? You must be a lucky guy, no enemies."

"And you must be a total jackass if the thought of not having any enemies seems somehow ludicrous to you," Jonas said.

"Oh, I'd say you have an enemy, Mr. Uhrig. A very nasty one. Beat up your housekeeper, trashed your home, stole your computer. There must be hundreds of thousands of dollars damage here. The insurance company won't be pleased. Who would do that?"

Jonas gritted his teeth. "If I knew that, I would have told you."

"Unless you're into something you don't want us to know about," the detective said, raising an eyebrow.

"Oh, for the love of…" Jonas ran his hands through his hair. "Isn't there supposed to be someone playing good cop? I think you're missing half the game here."

"You think this is a game?"

"I think you're being purposely obtuse," Jonas said.

"Obtuse?"

"Yes. Obtuse. I'd get you a dictionary, but seeing as how my house is trashed, I really don't think I'll be able to offer you the courtesy."

"You know what I think?" Detective Hernandez asked.

"No, but I'll bet it's full of melodrama, angst, and very little plot."

"I think you got yourself into some mess and now you're paying the price for it. Maybe drugs, maybe women, maybe something stickier."

"That's quite a story," Jonas said. "But it would never fly. Way too cliché. Try throwing in an element of the unusual or a few dancing bears. People love dancing bears."

"You think you're smart?"

"Nah. I just use my brain recklessly. Was that all, Detective, or did you have some other special little gems to share with me that you figured out with the help of a few late night 'Murder, She Wrote' episodes?"

"You're only making this harder on yourself."

"It's one of my special charms. My mum told me so when I was a boy. Mum would never have lied to me."

❦   ❦   ❦

After seeing a disgruntled Detective Hernandez off, and the forensics team had gotten enough blood samples to feed a small family of hungry vampires, Jonas had called to have the house cleaned and the locks changed. He gave Burke a bath and then salvaged what he could and had them throw away what was beyond repair. The pieces of his mother's beloved chandelier lay in a box in the dining room. He didn't think it could be fixed, but there was a possibility he could have one made from the pieces that were left.

When the cleaning crew was gone, he looked around at the emptiness. It no longer felt like home. It felt alien and menacing. He knew he was leaving tonight; he just wasn't sure where he was going yet.

Burke lay curled up on the rug in front of the door. He seemed to know it was time to go. Jonas went upstairs and tried not to think about what he would do when he finally had to come back again. He took another shower to wash away the dirt and blood that had clung to him over the past several hours of sorting through the mess. Afterward, he dressed in jeans and his favorite Ralph Lauren sweater. He packed up what clothing was left undamaged, though he planned on buying new ones at the first opportunity. He spotted the jasmine candles on the floor, and scooped them up, setting them gently in his bag before closing it.

He went to the phone and tried calling Raiden, but he didn't answer. This usually meant that he was in the middle of seducing some fine looking woman, so Jonas left a message to tell him he was leaving town, but that he'd keep in touch.

He'd been more than a little disappointed that Raiden hadn't answered. He needed that connection, that bond. Raiden had a way of making things seem okay, even in the worst of times.

When he returned downstairs, he found Burke standing at the door, his expression both solemn and hopeful.

"Ready to go?"

Chuff.

Jonas opened the door and stepped out into the cool twilight. The wind whispered softly through the trees. He opened the passenger door for Burke and stopped cold. There, on the tan leather seat lay his laptop. It was in sleep mode to reserve battery energy. Jonas fished around in the pocket of the back seat and found the auto power chord and stuck it in, bringing the laptop back to full power. On the screen was a message.

I am Horus, the great Falcon upon the ramparts of the house of him of the hidden name. My flight has reached the horizon. I have passed by the gods of Nut. I have gone further than the gods of old. Even the most ancient bird could not equal my very first flight. I have removed my place beyond the powers of Seth, the foe of my father Osiris. No other god could do what I have done. I have brought the ways of eternity to the twilight of the morning. I am unique in my flight. My wrath will be turned against the enemy of my father Osiris and I will put him beneath my feet in my name of 'Red Cloak'

"Whoever it is, Burke, they're crazy as a loon."
Chuff.
Jonas put the laptop in the backseat and motioned Burke to get in. The retriever hopped in and panted happily. Jonas put his bag in the trunk and slipped into the car.
"So, where we goin', pal?"
Chuff.
"Philadelphia it is, then."

CHAPTER 5

When Jonas arrived at the Radisson in King of Prussia, Pennsylvania four hours later, he was near exhaustion. He could have stopped anywhere along the road, but he was intent on getting as close to Philadelphia as possible. When he had called the Radisson for reservations and found that they had the Pharaoh's Tomb suite available after a cancellation, it was too laughably coincidental to pass up.

He checked in, leaving a generous deposit so there were no complaints about his four-legged companion and made his way to the room with Burke. Though he had stayed at this hotel several times, he had never stayed in any of the eighteen fantasy suites. Everything from Caesar's Palace to a Russian Ice Castle was available for the more whimsical customers, though they were usually booked solid.

He opened the door and stared for a moment. The room was an amazing blend of blacks, golds and tans, faux stone walls, intricately painted hieroglyphics and Egyptian figures of all sizes. A large falcon graced one wall, wings outspread. He had the sinking suspicion that it was Horus, but he wasn't well versed in Egyptian mythology and culture beyond what he had learned in school, so he couldn't be sure. Nevertheless, it made him slightly uneasy.

Burke curled up on the floor at the foot of the bed and napped, seemingly unmoved by the imagery. Jonas changed into jogging pants and a T-shirt and brushed his teeth while staring at a painting of Anubis. He wasn't sure how he knew it was Anubis, but figured that some of his ancient history classes had sunk in somewhere along the way.

He went over the message left on his laptop in his head as he climbed into the large golden bed. It was clear that he was going to have to do some brushing up on Egyptian mythology just to understand the implications of the message. It was also clear that whoever had trashed his apartment had also left the laptop in his car without triggering the alarm. That in itself was quite a trick. The person must also have had some knowledge of computers to be able to get past the password protection.

Either there had been more than one person behind the destruction of his home, or he hadn't been injured very badly despite the blood all over the bedroom that would seem to indicate otherwise. It seemed impossible to him that anyone could lose that much blood and still be able to walk, but he had heard of stranger things in his fourteen years of crime reporting.

He stared up at the ceiling, the soft glow of light from the bathroom illuminating just enough so that he could see the hieroglyphs on the wooden beams that ran across the ceiling. From among the various symbols, the Eye of Horus stared back at him. The longer he stared at it, the more certain he became that the symbol should mean something to him. Something more than a marker left by a murderer.

When viewed on a medium other than the crimson fabric of the scarf, the symbol seemed entirely different. It did not carry with it a feeling of evil or gloom, but one of protection and wholeness.

What significance did this symbol hold for the killer? It could be related to some sort of occult, Jonas thought. Though the murders lacked any sort of ritual elements, it couldn't be discounted.

He tried to recall any detail he could about the shadowy figure he'd glimpsed fleeing the alleyway, but there was only an impression of utter darkness in his mind. The entire alley had been cast in strange shadows thrown by the streetlamps on either side, but it had been enough to make out Belladonna's pink dress. His memory of the attacker was absolutely black, as if not just bathed in shadows, but as if he were darkness itself.

CHAPTER 6

❁

"We haven't had any new leads," Sergeant Cole said. He sat behind his desk, slightly slumped over, as if the weight of the world were truly on his shoulders. His dark hair was unkempt, though his uniform was immaculately pressed and neat.

Jonas didn't think the sergeant was more than a few years older than himself, which would put him in his late thirties, but he seemed tired. Not the sort of tired you get after a long day, but the tired that grows over time and seems to permeate every cell of your body.

"What about the scarf?" Jonas asked.

"We thought that might help. It was really our only link to the killer, but turns out those scarves are sold at hundreds of department stores. Forensics couldn't get anything off it except a few of the victim's own hairs.

"It was just a plain old scarf then? Why would the killer leave a simple red scarf?"

"Oh it wasn't that simple. Had a design on it. Some kind of eye. Our boys tried to take that angle, but it never turned up a thing. Such a damn waste. Pretty little girl like that with her whole future ahead of her. Damn waste."

"What sort of eye?" Jonas asked, his heart suddenly thudding in his chest.

"Our boys at the lab said some kind of Egyptian mumbo jumbo. Don't really recall the name at the moment, but it didn't pan out. The design was hand sewn onto the scarf with thread you could buy at any fabric store in town. You aren't the only one still wondering. Had some photographer here earlier wanting pictures of the scarf."

"Really? Who?"

"Woman named Kate Barnett. Couldn't let her see it though. It's our only evidence right now. Got to keep it locked up."

"Understandable," Jonas said. He knew the woman by her work, but had never met her. She was one of the best crime photographers in the field, and was reportedly more than slightly eccentric. He wondered why she was asking questions about the scarf. He supposed it could be coincidence, but the number of coincidences in this case were building up to an unbelievable level.

"Wish I had more to tell you. Hell, I wish I could say we caught the bastard," the sergeant said wearily.

"So do I," Jonas said. "Thanks for your time, Sergeant Cole."

"Not a problem. Maybe this story of yours will stir up some more interest and maybe someone out there knows something. Maybe we'll get a real lead." For the first time since Jonas had entered the man's office, he seemed to brighten.

"Maybe. It happens a lot. Let me know if you hear anything."

"Will do if I can."

Jonas shook the man's hand and left the office, taking in the familiar sights and sounds of the police department as he made his way to the front door. Endless movement, hushed phone conversations, the constant clicking of fingers flying over keyboards, the smell of old coffee and take-out food. The last reminded him that he was hungry, and Burke would likely be ready for lunch as well.

He found Burke sitting in the driver's seat, staring forlornly out the open window. It was a cool day and Jonas knew Burke wouldn't leave the car, so he had decided to bring him along.

"You driving?" Jonas asked.

Burke rolled his eyes and scooted to the passenger seat.

"Didn't think so. I always have to do the work around here."

Chuff.

"Ready for lunch?"

Chuff.

"I think I want some Italian. Extra meatballs for you."

Burke panted.

"Don't drool on the seat, pal," Jonas said with a smile.

❋   ❋   ❋

After picking up some take-out, Jonas and Burke went back to the hotel room. As Burke gulped down an alarming number of meatballs Jonas hooked the computer up to the phone line. There was no email from Rob Woo yet. Jonas hoped that meant he was sorting through a pile of results and not that there were no results to be found.

Jonas decided to do a web search on Kate Barnett. He found several news clippings with her photographs attached. He scanned through them. Her work was good. Better than most he had seen. She had a way of capturing moments that spoke clearly for themselves. The most recent photo was attached to a story on a killing in Cincinnati two days ago. The very day he had left the city.

The picture showed several officers behind a line of crime scene tape. One of them held a scrap of red in his gloved hand. Jonas scanned the article.

A sixty-eight year old man had been stabbed several times, his eyes cut out of his head. He died four hours later at the hospital while undergoing emergency surgery. The only clue left at the scene had been a red scarf. Police were unsure if it had been there prior to the attack or if it had been left by the assailant. No further description was given.

Jonas right-clicked on the picture and saved it to his hard drive and then opened it up with an imaging program. He enlarged the picture to three hundred percent and scrolled in to the scarf. The image was fuzzy, but he could see a black curved line in the center of the red.

Jonas's phone rang, startling him. He fished the small phone out of his pocket and answered.

"Uhrig."

"Hi. My name is Kate Barnett and I'm a freelance photographer. I had some questions about a couple of cases you covered and I was wondering if we could get together and chat. I'm just a few hours away from Richmond and..."

"No need. I'm in Philadelphia, too. Just saw Sergeant Cole this morning about the little girl who was killed. I can meet you at Valley Forge in an hour."

"Great. On my way. I'll be dressed in jeans and a red sweater. See you there."

As Jonas hit the end button and replaced the phone in his pocket, he was struck once more by the feeling that he knew, somewhere deep in his subconscious, what exactly was happening and how the pieces fit together.

Having finished his meal, Burke trotted over and laid his chin on Jonas's knee in a very unsubtle attempt to get his neck scratched. Jonas obliged, trying to sort his thoughts as he did so.

"Want to go for a walk?"

Chuff.

"I think we could both use the exercise. We have to see a lady about a scarf. I'm going to take a shower and then wipe the marinara off your furry face and then we'll get a move on."

🍁   🍁   🍁

Kate climbed out of her SUV, turning to dig around for pen and paper behind the seat before grabbing her camera. The late afternoon was cool and cloudy and the park was nearly empty. She pushed her bangs away from her face for the fourteenth time in five minutes and then walked to the main gate and sat on a bench just outside to await Jonas Uhrig.

She knew him only by reputation and from reading his work and both seemed to be flawless. She had heard rumors that he was not only handsome, but very probably gay. Of course, the latter she had heard from Lisa Carthridge so the reliability was very low. Lisa was a blonde bombshell and a reporter for the Times Dispatch. When Jonas had turned her down for a date, she had probably decided he was gay on principle rather than hard facts, just as she did most of her reporting. It didn't matter. Kate wasn't here to crawl in the sack with him. She was here to find out what he knew about the scarf.

She spotted a man with a dog crossing the street. He certainly fit the description she'd been given of Jonas. Tall, shoulder length black hair, dark skin, and a body that could only have been a gift from the gods. *He was probably a jerk*, Kate thought.

She stood as he approached, and though his demeanor was serious, he smiled briefly in greeting.

"You're Kate?" he asked. She wasn't what he expected. Her voice on the phone had been smooth and sophisticated. The woman before him was dressed in faded jeans and a baggy sweater, and what appeared to be very scuffed combat boots. Her hair was drawn back into a ponytail, and wisps of dark hair trailed down her neck and over her cheeks, framing her delicate features. The camera dangling around her neck gave her away, however.

"Yep. For twenty-nine years now. At least, that's the story my parents gave me. I haven't been able to verify that."

"I would be suspicious. Did you have them interrogated?"

"Certainly. But even under severe torture, they refused to give up the real story. Who's you're friend?" Kate asked, indicating the border collie who was panting happily at Jonas's side.

"This is Burke. He doesn't bite. Much. But unless you have a cheeseburger hidden on you anywhere, I think you're safe."

"Good to know," Kate said. She winked at Burke and was graced with a grin.

They began walking through the park as Kate continued, Burke electing to walk beside Kate, eyeing her adoringly.

"I think he's in love," Jonas sighed.

"He's got great taste," Kate smiled, bending to rub his head. Burke licked her hand affectionately and grinned.

"I can't argue."

"I know this was kind of sudden," Kate said. "But there was a case in Cincinnati a few days ago where they found a red scarf at the scene. I thought I recognized it, so I did some digging and came up with four more. Three of the stories were yours and I thought maybe you'd know something about it."

"Just a few hours after the killing in Cincinnati, there was a similar assault in Richmond where a red scarf was found," Jonas said. "The victim is still alive, but just barely. The attacker was interrupted, so he didn't get to finish the job."

"Was there anything on the scarf? A design?" Kate asked. "It would have been in black thread and shaped like…"

"The Eye of Horus," Jonas finished.

"So you saw it?"

"Yes, I saw it."

"What are the chances that the same guy killed someone in Cincinnati and then just a few hours later he assaults someone in Richmond?" Kate asked.

"I'm not sure. Low, I would think. But the chances of two totally unrelated crimes occurring where a red scarf was found with a delicately hand-embroidered symbol sewn into it are even lower. Either there is more than one assailant and they're working together, or our guy moves quick. I think it's the latter."

"Why?"

"Call it a hunch," Jonas said.

"Is that why you're here?"

"Yes," Jonas said. "If you knew the scarf had the symbol on it, why didn't the reporter put it in her story?"

"I actually didn't see it until I'd developed all the film. I don't know why I didn't give them that picture. I just had to see what I could find out first. It was like I knew the symbol would be there. As if I was searching for it."

"Photographer turned reporter?" Jonas asked.

"Gods, no," she said with a laugh. "Call it curiosity or impulse, but I'm no reporter. My photos tell the stories."

"You said you found four other cases. What was the fourth?"

"Tahoe last spring. A couple of tourists from Australia were stabbed to death. The scarf was found on the male victim. I don't know if the guy was the intended target and the wife just got in the way or if the killer targeted both of them," Kate said.

Jonas froze for a moment. He had been in Tahoe last spring. He had been in Cincinnati, he had been at the three other cities where the assaults occurred, and he had been in Richmond the night Bell was attacked.

"What is it?" Kate asked.

"Nothing. Killing a couple isn't his usual modus operandi. Wonder why he changed it."

"I don't know," Kate said. "But he's hardly selective when it comes to victims. He's an equal opportunity killer."

"Do you remember the date on the Tahoe murders?"

"No, but I have the articles in my Bronco if you want to have a look."

"Yeah. Maybe something in them will pop out at me."

They made their way to the parking lot. Kate's bright red Bronco was one of only three vehicles. When Jonas glanced inside, he saw that the back was full of clothes, papers, folders, boxes of various shapes and sizes, and other miscellaneous junk.

"You live in this thing?" he asked.

"Yep," she said as she dug through the backseat for the article.

"You're kidding."

"Nope. I've lived in it for two years now. I have to stay on the move so much that it really isn't worth paying rent or a mortgage somewhere. Aha!" Kate produced three slightly crumpled printouts and passed them to Jonas.

The date on the article was April 13th, the murders had occurred just after dark on the 12th. Jonas smothered a curse. He had been in Tahoe from the 5th to the morning of the 13th when he took a redeye flight to Burbank. This was more than a coincidence, but he had no idea what it meant.

"The park is about to close," Kate said. "Want to go grab some coffee?"

"Sounds good. Can we swing across to the hotel first so I can get my laptop? I thought we could compare this one with the others."

"Sure. Let me move some stuff around and I'll give you a lift." Kate took a large handful of various papers and other items and put them in the back and then shoved a large pile of junk over in the backseat so Burke would have room. Jonas wondered how she ever found anything in all the clutter.

"Climb in," she said.

❦ ❦ ❦

Kate parked in front of the Radisson and waited with Burke while Jonas went to retrieve his laptop. When he walked through the lobby a few minutes later, he saw several people standing in line to check in. Among them was a family with a little girl, no more than five years old who looked up at him and smiled, giving a little wave. Jonas waved back and her eyes sparkled with mirth at her game. The deep blue of her eyes reminded Jonas of stories of elves and fairies.

Jonas smiled and headed out the door to the Bronco. He found Burke sitting in the front seat, his head on Kate's lap. A clap of thunder split the air. Burke flinched at the sound and then nuzzled closer to Kate.

"He must have it bad," Jonas winked.
"Yes, but he's a perfect gentleman."
Chuff.
"Alright, mutt. Back you go," Jonas said.
Whine.
"The lady has to drive."

Burke sighed, but did as he was told. He sat directly behind Kate, leaning his head over her shoulder.

"Nothing like an adoring suitor to get a lady's self-esteem glowing," Kate laughed.

"He's apparently quite the Romeo. I never knew he had it in him." Jonas eyed Burke. "Next he'll be insisting on chocolates and flowers."

"Can't go wrong with flowers," Kate said. "And chocolate is rarely refused."

They pulled away from the hotel, heading for the coffee shop. Just as they left the parking lot and started down the road, the hotel exploded in a burst of flame, The Bronco rocked as the force of the blast overtook them. Debris smashed into the vehicle, shattering a rear window.

"Shit," Jonas said.

He opened the door and got out, turning to look at the remains of the hotel. He stood outside the SUV unable to move, staring at the destruction in front of him. He wasn't sure how long he stood there, but he was brought out of his daze when the sounds of sirens filled the air as emergency vehicles from all over the city approached at high speed. Kate had gone nearer to the scene to take pictures of the wreckage, Burke close at her heels.

The entire building had exploded, leaving nothing but a flat plane of wreckage spanning several blocks. Nothing was left standing. A large gaping chasm now dwelt where the building had once stood. There was no need to look for survivors. There couldn't possibly be any that he could get to with his bare hands. He looked toward the parking lot where his Maxima was now demolished under tons of debris.

In his mind, all he could think about was the family he'd passed in the lobby. The little girl with fairytale eyes. Dead. The light of wonder and gaiety in her eyes now extinguished, never to be seen again. So many people instantaneously ripped from the world. Why? Why the hotel? It certainly didn't qualify as a good terrorist target.

Suddenly, and with alarming clarity, Jonas knew that the bomb had been meant for him. Not to kill him, but for him to witness. The thought of someone blowing up an entire building and killing hundreds of people just to get at him might have seemed ludicrous only hours before. Now, however, he was either completely paranoid, or he was being hunted. Whoever had set the bomb could still be in the area.

"Kate!" Jonas yelled above the rising sirens.

She turned. "Just a minute!" she shouted back.

"No! Now, Kate! We have to get out of here!"

Either she was done taking pictures, or something in his voice told her the situation was extremely dire, because she turned and started running back to him. Burke followed, also seeming to sense the need for urgency.

"What's going on?" Kate asked.

"No time. Just get in and drive."

Kate nodded, fishing her keys out of her pocket and getting into the Bronco. Jonas opened the door for Burke and then climbed in the SUV.

"Drive," he said.

Kate accelerated slowly at first. Then, when she reached the main highway, she stepped on the gas. "What the hell is going on, Jonas? Ever since we met, you've been keeping something from me and I want to know what it is. And why the hell a journalist on the scene of a major catastrophe would choose to leave."

"It's complicated," Jonas said, turning to look out the opening where the back window had been blown out.

"Great. I have all the time in the world."

"You're going to think I'm crazy," he said.

"I already think you're crazy."

"You'll probably kick us out of your Bronco and run screaming to the cops."

"Nah. I might kick you out, but I'd never abandon the dog. Besides, the cops are going to be busy enough," she said.

Chuff. Burke said, grinning.

"I'm not sure I believe it myself."

"I don't doubt it. You strike me as the type who could shake hands with a little green alien and fly around in his spaceship and still try to gloss it over as some sort of delusion."

"You believe in aliens?" Jonas asked.

"Of course."

"Figures."

"Do you believe in a god?" she asked. Burke cocked his head to one side, and pricked an ear up, seemingly waiting for Jonas's reply.

"No," he said. "But you do, of course."

"I believe in more than any sort of god. There must be more."

"More than God? Boy, when you go for fantasy, you go big time." Jonas scratched Burke behind the ears, leaning in as if to share some secret. "No simple god for the lady here, Burke. She wants more."

"And you believe in nothing at all."

"That isn't true," Jonas said. "I believe in good beer and a rousing game of hockey."

"Spill it, Jonas."

As they drove through the deepening night, Jonas told Kate everything that had happened since he arrived back in Richmond. She was quiet as he told the tale, not interjecting or asking questions. Burke made little noise as well, only whining softly when Jonas spoke of Belladonna. When he finally finished by telling her his suspicions about the hotel explosion being meant for him, he sat awaiting her reaction.

Kate was silent, staring out at the road ahead as she drove. Jonas tapped his fingers against his knee.

"So?" he asked.

"Yeah," Kate said.

"So, do you think I'm crazy?"

"No. I have to think. It all fits."

"It does?" Jonas asked.

"Mhmm."

"How?"

"I don't know. It just does. It feels right, doesn't it? It can't all be coincidence."

"No, but if I've been in all the places where the killings and assaults have happened…"

"Then the police will think you did it," Kate finished. "So we obviously can't go screaming to them."

"And you aren't afraid I'll hack you to pieces?"

"Nope."

"Why?"

"The dog," Kate said.

"Burke?"

"Yes. He likes you. He trusts you. Animals are a very good judge of character."

"So you're basing your personal safety on the fact that my dog likes me?"

"Yep."

"Isn't that a little chancy?"

"Not at all."

Jonas looked back at Burke, the dog was grinning. "I think you're both nuts."

"Then you fit right in," Kate said.

"Where are we going anyway?"

"There's a nice little camping spot just southwest of Harrisburg. We can get a cabin for the night and figure out what to do in the morning."

※　　　　　※　　　　　※

Reamun followed the Bronco from a distance, often losing sight of the vehicle. If Jonas had no reason to be paranoid before, he most certainly was now. The appearance of the woman intrigued Reamun. She had been a surprise and Reamun was rarely surprised. He wondered who she was and how she fit in, or if perhaps she was just a temporary addition to the picture.

He was not displeased with this development even though it did not fit with his original plans. If the woman stayed and had a part to play, it would make things all the more interesting. He would have to watch her closely. If she turned out to be an obstacle, he would have to kill her.

For now, he would continue to watch and to wait. It wasn't yet time to bring Jonas into the fold.

CHAPTER 7

❀

The small cabin sat in a secluded spot overlooking a valley in the mountains. Jonas breathed deeply of the clean mountain air as he walked up the steps. They had paid more to have a cabin set apart from the others, the desk clerk smiling knowingly as he handed them the keys. Neither Jonas nor Kate corrected his false assessment of the situation. They wanted as little attention drawn to themselves as possible.

Kate unlocked the front door and Burke scrambled in before her, sniffing the room with doggy appraisal.

"Not bad," Jonas said.

"I like it. Certainly better than a stuffy hotel room," Kate said.

"You've obviously never stayed in the Pharoah's Tomb. Quite comfortable. Of course, it's now lying in a million tiny pieces on the ground of King of Prussia."

"It sounds macabre," Kate said. "Just my thing."

"It would be."

Kate smiled. "Only if there were mummies involved."

"You're a piece of work," Jonas said, trying not to dwell on the horrors of the last twenty-four hours. "Want some coffee?"

"Yes, please. If you don't mind, I'm going to hook up to the Net and see what fascinating things I can find on Egyptian mythology."

"Knock yourself out."

While Kate set up the laptop, Jonas made coffee and put together some sandwiches from the few groceries they had stopped to get along the way. He wondered again why Kate trusted him, and then it occurred to him that he trusted her as well. He wasn't sure that he should given the circumstances. Maybe it was Burke. Canine mind control, Jonas thought and smiled. All the craziness over the past few days had made him start seeing things where there was nothing to see. Burke was just a dog. The killer was only a man. Men made mistakes, and he meant to be there when this killer fouled up.

Chuff.

Jonas looked down to see Burke staring longingly at the turkey slices in his hand. "Alright, but just a few slices. We have proper dog food for you."

Burke gulped down the two slices of turkey while Jonas filled a small bowl with dog food and another with water. He poured the coffee and took a cup to Kate.

"Find anything interesting yet?" he asked as he set the cup down on the table beside her.

"A bit. There are a lot of different versions of the mythology. It seems to have evolved over time. Basically, Horus was either the son of Isis and Osiris or their brother, depending on which version you go with. He embodied kingship, sky and solar symbolism, and victory. There was a great battle between him and the god Set, or Seth, who killed his father. Seth was the god of chaos and seems to embody hostility and even outright evil. He is also a god of war, deserts, storms, and foreign lands. The wars between them lasted a long time. Some stories say Horus was victorious, others say that the final battle of good verses evil has not yet taken place. It is said that some day Horus will be victorious and on that day, Osiris and the rest of the gods will return to the earth."

"And the eye?" Jonas asked.

"It is associated with regeneration, health, and prosperity. It is also called the udjat eye or utchat eye, which means 'sound eye.'

Horus was called 'Horus who rules with two eyes.' His right eye was white and represented the sun; his left eye was black and represented the moon. According to myth, Horus lost his left eye to Seth during battle when Seth tore out the eye but lost the fight. Thoth reassembled the eye with magic. Thoth was the god of writing, the moon, and magic. He was also Horus's son.

"When used as an amulet, the Eye of Horus has three versions: a left eye is the moon, a right eye is the sun, and two eyes making 'The Two Eyes of Horus the Elder'. The eye is constructed in fractional parts, with 1/64 missing, a piece Thoth supposedly added by magic. The eye served to ensure safety, protect health, and give the wearer wisdom and prosperity, but also terror and wrath. It was called the 'all-seeing Eye'. According to some myths, the eye took on a personality of its own, swooping down out of the sky to right wrongs."

"Other than the whole search for victory and the terror aspect, it doesn't seem like the killer would identify with Horus. Strange," Jonas said.

"Yes," Kate said, sipping her coffee. "Maybe he doesn't identify with him. Maybe he's taunting you with the eye symbol."

"What about the message on the laptop? It said he was Horus."

"Unless he wasn't the one who left the message."

"Who else would have done that?" Jonas asked. "That would require the addition of another person into the scenario and Occam's razor would indicate otherwise. The simplest explanation being that the killer left the message."

Kate stared into her mug. "I'm not sure."

"Your turn to spill it, Kate."

She looked up at him, meeting his gaze only briefly. "I'm not sure. I'm still thinking. It seems to me that the killer would identify with Seth. He's certainly one for chaos and hostility."

"I agree, but why all the Horus symbolism if he thinks he's Seth, or a warrior for Seth?" Jonas asked.

Kate looked at him once more, this time holding his gaze. Burke had stopped eating and had come quietly in the room and was now seated at Kate's feet. He also looked at Jonas.

"You're right," Kate said after a moment. "It doesn't make much sense right now. We need to think it through and get some more research done. But right now we need food and sleep. We'll think more clearly in the morning."

Jonas felt that she knew something he didn't, but he let it pass. If she was reluctant to say, it was most likely because it was preposterous. When a woman who believed in aliens and left her safety in the judgment of a dog thought something was preposterous, it was best to sleep on it.

🍁   🍁   🍁

I lay in a bed of cool dry leaves, watching the forlorn full moon as it makes its way across the sky, so sure in its path. The wind picks up; cool night air caresses my naked flesh. It soothes me. I am alone, as I have been most of these long years.

I close my eyes, blocking the view of the solitary orb. I let my mind drift, searching for the Other. It takes me longer than usual to find my enemy. He is growing more powerful every day. His mind is becoming sharper, attempting to protect him from intrusion.

His meager defenses are not enough to cause me much trouble yet, however. There is still time. I concentrate on my enemy, I feel the fear and doubt there. Our bond is a strong one and I am surprised that the Other does not feel it as acutely as I do. I am able now to see him for the first time. Always before I could but feel his emotions and sense the path of his thoughts. Now I am with him. He is completely oblivious of my presence in that dark cabin room with him.

I can feel the silken strands of his long ebony hair that fan out on the pillow. I feel the taut muscles that flow so gracefully through my enemy's body. I can feel the tightening of loins as the Other dreams of the woman. Though my mind is there with him, it is not enough.

I want to see him before me as he is now with my own eyes, not as images in my mind.

Suddenly, another presence is there in the room with us. This one feels my presence clearly. It drives me out and away. Back to my bed of leaves beneath the stars.

I open my eyes. The moon has passed beyond the opening in the canopy of trees above me. Though the cold orb no longer stares down at me, I can still see the mournful glow through dark branches.

CHAPTER 8

❀

Jonas stood in a vast barren land, faraway sand dunes the only relief from the flat emptiness around him. He felt a presence, something vile and evil. He turned, scanning the endless plane, but saw nothing. In the distance, a slow wailing began. Softly at first, but then he recognized it as cries of grief. A child's cries. They seemed to come from everywhere and nowhere at once.

He felt warmth rise up from the sand at his feet. Rivers of blood swelled up around him. He fought to swim, to keep his head above the surface, but the thick oozing liquid churned around him, pulling him under. The more he struggled, the further he seemed to be dragged under the tide. Finally, he went limp. Slowly his body rose to the surface. He was buoyant now, his body floating easily on crimson waves.

Slowly, the river diminished, vanishing back into the sand. He was left lying on the ground, staring up into the hot shimmering sun. Warmth flowed through him. A feeling of calm permeated his being. And then a black disk slowly drifted across the sky. As it moved across the surface of the sun, the warmth in his body was replaced with a cold so profound that he could associate it only with the chill of death.

All too soon, the light was completely extinguished, caught behind a veil of blackness. The darkness shifted around him. He could feel the presence more strongly now, coming nearer. He tried to move, to stand, but his legs were caught in the vice-like grip of scaly claws. A cold hand pressed against Jonas's throat, fingers pressing into his skin, cutting off the air supply. He struggled, frantically clawing at the hand on his neck to no avail. With one hand he reached out into the black void in front of his face. His hand met a cold long snout. A foul smell greeted Jonas as the thing opened its jaws revealing gleaming yellow shards of teeth. The gaping maw swooped down, tearing at his flesh. Jonas screamed.

🍁   🍁   🍁

Jonas woke with a start, a cold nose pressed to his hand. He reflexively pulled it away, panting in terror as he reached for the bedside lamp. Only it wasn't there. Jonas heard a soft whine, and he realized that it was Burke. He reached out a shaking hand, stroking the dog's head and the realization of where he was slowly came back to him. He was on the couch in the cabin. A soft glow came from the computer screen on the table. He was sheathed in sweat, his body shaking. He had tossed the covers to the floor at some point in his sleep. Burke whined again.

"It's okay, pal. Just a bad dream," Jonas said. He wasn't quite sure which one of them he was trying to reassure. "I thought you went to sleep with Kate. She snore?"

Burke made a disgusted noise, clearly indicating that she most certainly did not snore.

"Interspecies relationships rarely work, you know."

Burke rolled his eyes.

"Fine. Just don't say I didn't warn you, bud."

The idle chatter slowly calmed Jonas's body and mind. The cool night air washed over his bare torso as he stood, making him shiver. He went to the small kitchen and got a glass of water, gulping it down and filling the glass again. As he turned to look back at the living room, he remembered that he had turned the computer off before going to sleep.

With growing dread, he set the glass of water aside and approached the laptop. On the screen was another message.

O You who take away and bring days to an end, do not take away my years or bring my days to an end, for I am Horus, Lord of the All That is Seen, Ruler of the Western Horizon.

I will not die in the West, and the messengers of Ha have no power over me, for I am Horus, son of Osiris.

I will not die in the East, and the messengers of Sopedu have no power over me, for I am Horus, son of Osiris.

I will not die in the North and the messengers of the Outcast have no power over me, for I am Horus, son of Osiris.

I will not die in the waters, and the messengers of Nun have no power over me, for I am Horus, son of Osiris.

I will not die in the Abyss, and the messengers of Naunet have no power over me, for I am Horus, son of Osiris.

I will not die a second time, and the dwellers of All That is Seen have no power over me. I will not eat their fish. Their fowl shall not scream over me, for I am Horus, son of Osiris.

Jonas stood staring at the monitor for a very long time. How could anyone have come into the cabin without waking him? It was possible that Burke had not heard the intruder while sleeping in Kate's room, but how could someone have been in the very same room while Jonas was sleeping, start the computer, type the message, and then leave without waking him?

Jonas checked the time on the taskbar. It was four fifty-three. He had been asleep for five and a half hours, and yet he felt as if he had only just lain down. Jonas checked both the front and back doors of the cabin. Neither showed signs of forced entry and both were still securely locked. He checked the windows and found the same. His phone rang, and Jonas scrambled over to the coffee table where he had left it to charge.

"Uhrig."

"Hey, bro. Got your results. Just emailed 'em to ya," Rob Woo said.

"Do you ever sleep?" Jonas asked.

"When I'm tired."

"Did you find much?" Jonas asked.

"Yeah. I sorted them out into three zip files. First one has the most likely ones. Five killings and four brutal assaults. All had a red scarf left at the scene on or near the body. Some of them say it had some sort of markings on it. Second file has six murders where a scarf was found at the scene. Either they didn't mention the color, or the scarf wasn't that close to the body. Third file has a whole slew of cases where any type of scarf was put into the list of items taken from the crime scene."

"Thanks, Rob. I'll check the email."

"Heard anything about Bell?"

"No. I haven't had a chance to check on her since yesterday," Jonas said, guilt flooding through him.

"That's alright. I just called. Figured you were up to your neck in it. She isn't awake yet, but her vitals are good and her reflexes are working. Thought you'd want to know."

"Yeah, I did." Jonas looked up as Kate walked into the room, rubbing her eyes. She was dressed only in a tank top and boxers and it took all his strength of will not to stare.

"You need anything else?" Rob asked.

"No. Thanks. I'll let you know, though."

"Right on. Later."

Jonas hit the end button and looked up at Kate, forcing himself to look only at her face. "Did I wake you?"

"I heard the phone," Kate said. "I've been waking up every half hour or so anyway. Anything important?"

"Maybe. First you need to take a look at the computer." Jonas stood and walked over to indicate the words glowing on the monitor.

Kate's brow furrowed and then she turned to the computer, her eyes suddenly widening as she approached. She read the passage twice. Jonas watched as she mouthed the words on the screen.

"How did he leave the message?" Kate asked.

"I don't know. I was trying to figure that out myself. Unless I was just so deeply asleep that I didn't hear anyone come in. No signs of forced entry."

"Wouldn't Burke have made a ruckus if someone was in here?"

"Unless he didn't hear anything. He was in there with you and the door was closed," Jonas said.

"Did you let him out?"

"What?"

"He was in my room. The door was closed. How did Burke get out?"

Jonas looked at the dog who was resting peacefully on the rug in front of the couch. "I have no idea. It doesn't make any sense."

"Unless whoever left that message was someone he trusted, someone who let him out of my room," Kate said.

"So he's not such a good judge of character after all?"

"That isn't what I'm saying. I think he *is* a good judge of character. What if the person who is leaving these messages doesn't mean any harm?"

"I'm not following here."

"What if the person leaving the messages is on your side? Horus was all that is good and divine, the pharaohs were said to be the embodiment of Horus. If he is fighting evil and chaos and corruption, then he is essentially righteous."

"It wouldn't be the first time a serial killer thought he was a god, or some tool of the divine. It's just those sorts of delusions that spur them on. It gives them purpose and meaning and the drive to kill and maim and justify it all at the same time," Jonas said. "Maybe this guy thinks he's Horus and that all the people he is killing are enemies of Osiris."

"Why not kill us? Let's say for the sake of argument that Burke is a really bad judge of character. The guy comes in, checks my room, the dog gets out. He sits and types this message and then leaves. We could also say for the sake of argument that he left you alive so he could finish his little game. But why not kill me? Why not kill Burke? Or both of us?"

"Maybe he didn't have time," Jonas said. "Or maybe he was afraid of making too much noise. Who knows? But if he was on our side, why leave cryptic messages about Egyptian gods?"

Kate turned back to the computer screen, her back to him. "I don't know."

Jonas once again knew she was holding something back. He should ask her what it was that she didn't want to say. It could be important. She was obviously following some train of thought that made sense to her and it was one she was unwilling to reveal to him. He didn't ask.

"Let's check the email I got from Rob. He said he found several more cases. Maybe we'll get a better feel for where this is headed," Jonas said.

Kate made the coffee this time while Jonas downloaded the attachments of the email and opened the zip files, searching through the articles. As he read through them, his hands started shaking. He was only halfway through the second batch, but had already found nineteen cases that definitely fit the killer's pattern. Jonas had been in all those places at the times the murders and assaults had occurred.

He checked CNN's website for the latest news on the bomb at the hotel, and found there were still no suspects or leads. He didn't expect that there would be. Somehow he knew that this killer would not be caught by the police, the FBI, or any other law enforcement.

Again, he thought of the little girl in the lobby of the hotel. Had she been killed because of him? Because he had chosen that hotel?

Had they all been killed because of him? And if they had, how could he possibly live with that knowledge? He didn't think he could.

"Well?" Kate asked, returning with the coffee.

"Not good. Nineteen more cases so far, and I was in every city at the time they occurred. There are twelve other possibilities, but I'll have to check my records to verify. These go back fifteen years."

"What happened fifteen years ago? Why did it start then?" Kate asked

"I don't know. That's about the time I started my job as a freelance journalist, though one of the cases happened about six months prior to that."

"But you were there when it occurred?"

"Yes. I don't travel because of my job. I got the job as an excuse to travel. I'm never comfortable in the same spot very long. I have to keep moving."

"Bad case of wanderlust?"

"It's more complicated than that," Jonas said.

"Oh?"

Jonas shifted uneasily. He had never before explained to anyone about his need to roam, but knowing that it probably related to the case he decided to tell her. "It started shortly after my parents died seventeen years ago. I was eighteen when it happened. It's more of a *need* to get out than a simple urge or longing. It's hard to explain, but when I get that feeling, I have to leave. I have no choice."

"What about destinations? Do you just pick a place at random?"

"No. I usually have some place in mind. If I don't right off, then I usually have one by the time I get on the road or to the airport."

"So either he's following you or you're following him," Kate said.

"How could I be following him when I didn't even know he existed until a few days ago?"

"It isn't necessary for you to be consciously aware of him. You aren't consciously aware of what drives you to these places, so maybe you're drawn to him."

"That's a little far fetched," Jonas said.

"I don't think so. I think it makes perfect sense. You were somehow subconsciously aware of this guy. You knew when he was going to kill, so you went to those places. It would also explain why he hasn't gone after you before this. Maybe he only just found out about you as well."

"But if I knew, why didn't I ever try to stop him?"

"Because you weren't consciously aware of it. And perhaps though you knew the general location of the crime to be committed, you didn't know enough of the details to keep it from happening."

"Not only does your theory contain a lot of ifs, but it requires a belief in some kind of psychic ability. I'm not psychic," Jonas said flatly.

"I've seen you talk to Burke. You know what he's thinking. He knows what you're thinking. And you don't even speak the same language."

"People talk to their dogs all the time."

"Not like you talk to Burke, and dogs don't normally follow conversation so well."

"He's smart," Jonas said.

"Yes, he's very smart, but that doesn't fully explain it. You have conversations with your dog, Jonas. Ones in which he is a full participant. Hasn't that ever struck you as odd?"

Jonas shook his head. "I think you're making more of this than there really is. Burke would also have to be telepathic for this little scenario to work out."

"Uh huh."

"A telepathic dog?" Jonas asked.

Kate nodded.

"Telepathic dogs and little green men from outer space. Is there anything you don't believe in?"

"Coincidence," Kate said.

❦   ❦   ❦

I awake as the sun rises, dawn lighting the canopy of trees with golden fire. I run my hands over my bare torso and find that my wounds have fully healed. I am pleased that it hasn't taken long. My body is capable of swift regeneration now. I can feel the powers coursing through my veins.

Though I had still been recovering from my wounds yesterday, the explosion of the hotel had given me a surge of energy like nothing I had experienced before.

In that moment, I felt the utter terror of the Other. I tasted the bile that rose in his throat, heard the pounding of his heart. He is ever magnificent, but more so on the occasions when he is in the grip of pure emotion.

Just a little longer and I will regain my full powers. This new era is full of chaotic energy, hate, and war. It feeds me, nourishes me, and with just a little effort on my part, I will be glorious and mighty as I once was, long ago.

I rise to my feet, gathering my clothes from the ground and dressing without haste. I will deal with the Other when the time is right. First I must separate my foe from those who will protect him and help him. This will serve to crush his confidence as well as to cut off many resources. As I slip my shirt on, I am struck with inspiration. Cambridge, Massachusetts. I am filled with a bright sense of anticipation.

❦   ❦   ❦

Jonas and Kate spent all morning searching through the articles. They cross-checked them with Jonas's travel diary, which he kept meticulously up-to-date. When they were finished, they had eighty-three cases involving a scarf that matched Jonas's travels.

"That's only about five per year," Kate said. "It doesn't feel like enough."

"But there could be more that we just haven't found. The police would probably overlook the scarf in many cases. Especially if the victims were women. And these only cover the killings in the U.S. and Canada. I do a great deal of traveling overseas. At least twice a year. Sometimes more."

Kate closed her eyes. "I don't want to think about it. How could the police have overlooked this for so long?"

"He moves around a lot. His victims don't seem to have anything in common, and the scarf isn't always prominent in the reports. The police probably wrote most of them off as random violence. The world is full of random violence and tragedy. Misery is unavoidable."

Kate opened her eyes and stared at him. "No it isn't. The world is full of beauty and wonder and *good*, Jonas. Sure, bad things happen and there are bad people in the world, but no matter how short a time we're here on Earth, we *choose* our path. Whether we live joyfully and with love of life or we live in sorrow and fear, it is a choice. A choice we can only make for ourselves."

"So you're saying 'Shit happens, but smile anyway'?" Jonas asked.

"Exactly. Don't dwell on the bad in life. If something is wrong you either fix it or learn to live with it. Whichever it is, you can only do so much. The bigger picture is much more important. The ecstasy of life, the very essence of it, *that* is something to revel in. Every day is full of wonder if you only know where to look."

"That sounds like a greeting card."

"You're impossible."

"So I'm told." Jonas flashed a grin. "Think I'll go take a shower and a short nap. We should probably follow up on some of these cases, but I don't feel like I slept a wink."

"Take the bedroom. I'll make some calls and do some more research and see what else I can come up with."

🍁   🍁   🍁

Reamun watched the cabin from his spot in the woods. He knew it wouldn't be long before they would be on the move again. Jonas was slowly becoming aware of the stakes, but he was still unsure of the goal. He knew only that he had to find and stop the person behind the seemingly random violence.

"There is so much more than that," Reamun whispered. "So much more."

Reamun knew that the messages Jonas had found on the laptop had frightened and confused the man, but they had also gotten his mind pondering possibilities. Possibilities he was not quite ready to face. He would learn soon enough. He must learn.

Reamun had also come to realize that the woman was far more than she seemed. She intuited much more than she should. He still had no idea who she was. He knew she was Kate Barnett, freelance photographer, age twenty-nine. But that meant nothing. He needed to know *who she was*. The fact that he couldn't get a sense for her disturbed him.

The dog, he decided, may not pose a risk as he had first thought. It was difficult to see, and though he had been helper in the past, it did not mean he was completely averse to switching sides. Battles such as these often changed the minds of even the most stalwart of allies. After all, hadn't this very war seen a mother turn against her son in the most shocking show of betrayal imaginable? Choosing between sires could prove to be a much more difficult choice.

Reamun's cell phone vibrated in his pocket.

"Yes?"

"Everything is ready," the woman said.

"Good."

"What is this all about? Why does the meeting need to be set up this way?"

"Just be certain nothing goes wrong. He will need to have everything just right," Reamun said.

"It is just as you wanted. I still don't understand."

"You don't have to."

"Why are you helping him? I thought…"

"Trust me. This will all work out to everyone's benefit in the end. Now go prepare. I will speak with you later."

Reamun hit the end button. After one last look at the cabin, he turned to head back down the forest trail to his waiting car.

🍁   🍁   🍁

Jonas woke two hours later, and knew he had to leave. The late afternoon sun sent beams of light through the window shades. He lay there for a moment and stared at the ceiling as he gathered his thoughts. It took him a moment to remember where he was and then the sense of urgency slammed into him.

He got up and dressed quickly in the same clothes he had worn the day before. He would have to stop to get some new clothes now that his entire wardrobe had been demolished in one way or another. It could wait. Right now he had to get to Massachusetts. He stumbled into the main room as he struggled to get his shoe on. Kate looked up from the computer, arching her brow.

"We have to get moving. Pack everything up," Jonas said.

Burke rose to his feet and went to sit beside the door as Jonas started gathering what food they could eat on the road.

"What's the hurry?" Kate asked.

"Don't know. We just have to get to Massachusetts. I think we can drive it if we go straight through. Should take no more than eight hours."

"Six if I drive," Kate said as she began packing up the laptop. "No idea why we're going?"

"No. I just…we have to be there by morning."

They were ready to go in little less than half an hour. They set off with Kate driving and Jonas looking at the map to determine the best route. Burke sat silently in the back seat staring out the window.

"The past few times he's targeted you, or someone close to you," Kate said. "Any idea what this could…"

"Rob," Jonas said, clear panic in his voice. "Rob Woo is in Cambridge. Shit." Jonas dug the cell phone out of his pocket and dialed Rob's number. There was no answer. Jonas left a message telling Rob to call him the minute he got the message. Jonas tried Rob's parent's house, but neither knew where their errant son had gotten to.

"He's probably at a bar or on some date with some girl who isn't any good for him," Erika Woo said. "He says he goes to the library. He thinks we're stupid. He didn't come home last weekend for family dinner, and you know what he told us?"

"No," Jonas said, trying to think of some polite way to end the conversation.

"He said he had the flu. I'm his mother. I've nursed him through many flu seasons, and he most certainly did not sound like a young man with the flu. Very bad actor. Good thing he chose a major in computer science, that one."

"I agree," Jonas said, smiling despite himself. "If you hear from him, could you have him call me? It's important."

"I'll tell him. Are you okay, Jonas?"

"Fine, Mrs. Woo. Just need some help with a computer problem that can't wait."

"You're no better at the lying than Rob is," she said with a laugh. "But I'll tell him you called."

Jonas ended the call, feeling frustrated.

"No luck?" Kate asked.

"No, but he doesn't usually stay out long. I'll keep trying. Hopefully he'll be back by the time we get there."

"Something's been bothering Burke," Kate said.

Jonas looked back at the dog. Having heard his name, he turned his attention away from the landscape as it flew past the window and met Jonas's gaze.

"I don't blame him," Jonas said. "A lot has been happening. He was there when I found Bell."

"Maybe. I don't know. He seems preoccupied, but you know him better than I do."

"Sometimes he's just quiet," Jonas said as he reached back to stroke Burke's head. "Probably daydreaming about steak or Frisbees."

Chuff.

"No steak tonight, pal. We may stop for a burger though."

Chuff.

"When this is all over, I promise I'll get you the biggest steak you can handle."

Burke panted, but Jonas could see that the dog was no better at lying than he was. Burke was worried about something.

Jonas thought about what Kate had said earlier. It seemed extremely unlikely, but perhaps it was more empathy than telepathy. They had been together every day for two years, that sort of time spent together would surely result in at least a simple understanding and ability to communicate.

CHAPTER 9

❀

Rob Woo was on his third martini of the evening. He wasn't sure why he was at this party, other than having promised his best friend he'd come along, but Ian had long ago abandoned him for a cute redhead. Now Rob was stuck between two mathematicians arguing about chaos.

He spotted Liv Sampson across the room and decided it was going to be his only real opportunity to extricate himself gracefully.

"Excuse me, I see a friend across the room. Catch you guys later." Neither of them seemed to notice his departure as they continued their argument.

Rob saw that Liv was clad in a deep red corset which showed off the edge of a vine-like tattoo on her breast as well as one with some sort of hieroglyphs on her arm, black leather skirt, and high heeled boots. He noted her hair color for the day was lavender. She never matched her hair color with her otherwise perfectly matching outfits. He wasn't exactly sure why, but he liked it.

He had been in lust with her since last semester, but held very little hope of ever doing anything about it. She was wild, a free spirit, a woman who knew what she wanted and how to get it. He was a hopeless computer geek who had trouble deciding what color socks to put on in the morning.

"Hey Bliss," he said, using her screen name, as was common among the computer crowd.

"Damn, Anarch. I thought you never came to these things," she said. She lit a cigarette and threw back her head as she downed a vodka shot.

"I was coerced under duress. You come to these things a lot?"

"Nah," Liv said sneering. "Mostly just come when I need to feel like I'm not the lowest scum on the earth. Look around. Lots of sad specimens here."

"It's supposed to be a party, but everyone is talking shop," Rob said. "It's a wonder anyone ever gets laid around here."

Liv laughed. "I'm afraid to see what the mating of any of these people would spawn." She shuddered in mock horror. "Speaking of which," Liv paused to down another vodka shot. "How come you never asked me out?"

"What?" Rob nearly spit out his drink. "I mean, you want me to?"

"Yeah, but you never have. It's the hair, isn't it?"

"I love your hair."

"The clothes?"

"Love the clothes."

"My overbearing personality?"

"I find it refreshing."

"Chemistry just not there?"

"I've wanted you since the first time I laid eyes on you," Rob said. The words were out before he could stop them.

"So you're chicken? I thought as much. Wanna go rent a cheesy movie and make out?"

"Are you ever subtle?"

"No," she said. "It wastes too much time. I would have asked you before, but I figured you needed time to adjust."

"Adjust?" Rob asked.

"To your rampant sexuality and your lust for someone who your parents would definitely not approve of," she said.

"My parents don't approve of anyone of the female persuasion."

"So, we going or not?"

"I thought you had a boyfriend. Some rock star looking guy is what Beth said. Tall, dark and handsome. She nearly swooned just talking about him."

"Oh, he's not interested in me," Liv said with a smile. "And Beth would swoon over anything in tight pants. I only see him when he's around, and that isn't often. Can we go?"

"Let me get my jacket," Rob said.

🍁 🍁 🍁

Reamun followed the Bronco north. Not much longer now. Just a matter of a few hours. He wondered what would happen when Jonas arrived. Would he figure it all out in time? Reamun doubted it. Jonas would lose this battle, but there were more battles to come. However, time was running out.

It would be interesting to see if Jonas figured it out before the end came. But by the time he did, he would have little time to be fully prepared. It would have been different if his parents had not sheltered him in the futile hope that they could keep the inevitable from happening. It was only after their deaths that his powers began to emerge, but so strong was the power of their teachings that he refused to see his own potential, his own quest. In the end, his parents' wish to protect him could prove to be the one that left Jonas as the perfect target.

🍁 🍁 🍁

Kate glanced at Jonas as he pretended to study the map. She shifted her eyes back to the road and wondered how long he could keep deluding himself. All the evidence was right there in front of him, and yet he couldn't see it because he was so enamored with the idea that everything in the universe had some rational order to it that he could look at from a contemporary logical point of view. She had the growing sense that time was running out, and yet she couldn't force him to see the truth. He had to come to his own conclusions. She just hoped he was able to figure it all out in time.

"Our exit is coming up," Jonas said. "He lives right off campus."

"And if he isn't there?"

"We'll just have to wait."

"Have you tried concentrating on the feeling? Tried to figure out where exactly you need to be?"

"I'm not psychic, Kate."

"Then why are we here?"

Jonas said nothing.

"If the killer is following you and not the other way around, won't we just be leading him to Rob?"

"He probably already knows about Rob. He went through all my things at the house."

"Probably? But you can't be sure. Jonas, you have to stop pretending that there isn't at least some element of the supernatural involved here."

He didn't say anything. Jonas didn't know what to say. He could explain a lot of it in bits and pieces in a logical fashion, but it required a great deal of coincidence to put it all together, and any good reporter knew that coincidences like these were rare. More than one was next to impossible. Burke stood on the back seat, leaning in to nudge Jonas's shoulder with his nose.

"Alright," he said finally. "I'll try, but only because Rob's life is at stake. Not because I believe in this crap."

"Fair enough."

He closed his eyes, feeling more than slightly idiotic, but he decided it couldn't hurt. He tried to reach to that place inside him, the urgent place that forced him to stay on the move. He tried to concentrate on the feeling. If he could only pick it apart and figure out why, he would have many of the answers, and he might just save Rob's life.

Suddenly, he felt someone else there inside him. Another entity. Fully aware and *alive* inside of him. The other reached out for him, ancient tendrils of memory attempting to wrap themselves around him. Jonas opened his eyes, gasping for breath as he lurched forward in his seat, breaking the tenuous contact.

"What is it?" Kate pulled the Bronco to the side of the road, leaning over to place a hand on Jonas's back. "Jonas?"

"I…" Jonas shook his head. The feeling was gone, but the memory was enough to make him shiver. "I don't know. Just go. We have to get to Rob."

"Jonas…"

"Go, Kate. Now."

Kate pulled off the shoulder and back onto the blacktop, but glanced repeatedly at Jonas who was leaned forward, staring out the windshield as if he had seen a ghost.

※　　　　※　　　　※

I stand in a candle lit room, surrounded by a soft luminous glow. I resist the urge to reach out to the Other. As much as I wish to know what is going on inside his mind and heart, I know that contact now might only lead him here. It wouldn't do to have him show up too soon.

Of course he knows something will happen, as he always knows. Yet he does not know enough to stop me. To do this, he would have to relinquish his hold on his humanity, which he is loathe to do. This intrigues me. I am constantly invigorated by his essence, by his sheer determination of will. This quality simultaneously hinders and aids him.

I slowly disrobe, folding each garment neatly on the dresser beside the bed. I lean against the wall, feeling the texture of the rough stone against my back. Closing my eyes, I center on the power within me.

My lips move as I began to whisper ancient words that will bring forth the energies I require to complete the task before me.

I hear voices in the other room, but I block them from my mind. Soon I will prove my greatness and I must be prepared.

※ ※ ※

Rob sat on the couch in the poshly furnished flat while Liv went into the kitchen for drinks. He supposed Liv's parents were rich. His family was more than just comfortable, but the intricately carved furnishings, soft fabrics, and artifacts lining the room were like nothing he had ever before seen, especially not in the dwelling of a university student.

Everything was immaculate and not a hint of dust was on any of the stone carvings. In a glass case on one wall was a golden figure. He was almost certain it was Egyptian in design. Though he knew it could not possibly be authentic, it looked as if it could have come straight from the tomb of an ancient pharaoh. Rob stood, crossing the room to get a better look. The figure was no more than eight inches in height, having the form of a human body with the head of what looked to Rob like an aardvark.

"You like him?" Liv asked, emerging from the kitchen and coming to stand beside Rob.

"It's beautiful," Rob said, taking the drink from Liv. "Where did you get this?"

"A friend," she said with a glib smile. "He is Seth, an Egyptian god. One of the most misunderstood gods, in my opinion."

"Misunderstood how?"

"He is said to be evil. He is held responsible for all sin and wrongdoing in the world. That would be quite a task, don't you think?"

"Busy guy," Rob said.

"But he was responsible for a great deal of good as well. He is the father of Djeheuty, the one the Greeks named Thoth. Everyone sought Thoth's council because he was wise and well-versed in the ways of magic. How could such good come from pure evil?"

"Depends on who the mother was," Rob said.

"Ah," Liv smiled. "But there was no mother. Thoth was the son of both Seth and Horus, the god of the sky. Horus and Seth were said to be enemies, and this is true, but it was not always so."

"Lovers quarrel?" Rob asked.

"Not so simple as that."

"It never is," Rob said, taking a sip of his drink. It was like nothing he had ever tasted before. Sweet and yet earthy, a perfect combination of flavors. "What's in this?"

"My special recipe. Drink up."

"So you're really into this Egyptian stuff?"

"Yes, I am. It fascinates me."

"Why not go into Egyptology then?"

"Most Egyptologists are fools and hacks," Liv said. "And the few who aren't are completely discounted by their colleagues. They're all blind."

"Why do you say that?"

"If we're to believe their version of Egyptian history, the entire civilization sprang up, fully formed, out of nowhere only a few thousand years ago. Their technology peaked shortly after this supposed appearance and then steadily declined from there. Does that make any kind of sense to you?"

"No," Rob said. "I don't suppose it does."

"But enough of that. Finish your drink and come with me. There's something I want you to see."

"Oh really? Where?"

"In the bedroom," Liv said.

Rob downed his drink in one long swallow. "Lead on."

Liv led him to the bedroom and opened the door, motioning for Rob to go first. He felt lightheaded. He grasped the doorframe and looked into the room. Figures seemed to shift and dance along the walls.

A single dark figure pushed away from the wall and approached Rob as if one of the drawings had merely sprung to life. Tall and graceful, the figure moved toward him. Rob could make out none of his features, but saw that he was naked. The man held out a hand to him.

"Who are you?" Rob asked, trying to clear his head.

"I am known by many names," the man said. His voice was smooth and sensuous. Rob was reminded of the myth of the Siren's call. He looked at the outstretched hand wreathed in shadow. The long tapered fingers were the most beautiful he had ever seen.

"I don't…understand," Rob said.

"You will." The man's voice was reassuring. "This will take very little time, and soon you will be filled with the light of the gods."

CHAPTER 10

❁

"Alright, Jonas," Kate said as they neared Rob's apartment building. "What happened back there?"

"Nothing," he lied.

"Something."

"My imagination."

"Tell me. I believe in little green men, remember? It isn't going to seem weird."

"Maybe I just don't want to encourage you," Jonas said.

"I promise that whatever it is, I won't blame it on aliens," Kate smiled.

"So you're going to blame it on my psychic dog?"

"Nah, he's too cute. Quit stalling, we're almost there."

Jonas looked at her and saw in her eyes that she wouldn't judge him, no matter how ludicrous the tale that came out of his mouth. Even if he thought himself crazy, she never would. He was again struck by that feeling that she knew something that he didn't. She seemed full of extraordinary knowledge and wisdom. He mentally berated himself for attributing fantastical qualities to the current situation.

"There was something...no, that's not right," Jonas said. "*Someone* inside of me. I felt this other being, this other entity. I could almost see his mind, but it freaked the hell out of me."

"His? Not her?" Kate asked. "Or it?"

Jonas paused for a moment. He had no idea how he had known the gender of the entity. "Yeah. Male."

"Was it the killer?"

"No," Jonas said. "I don't think so. He didn't seem evil, just insistent."

"What did he want?"

"I don't know. I think maybe he wanted me to remember something." Jonas was acutely aware that the entire conversation was absurd. He winced.

Kate nodded. "It makes sense."

"The hell it does. I was probably just imagining things."

"We're here," Kate said as she pulled the Bronco into the parking lot.

"Park over there," Jonas said. "I don't see his car, but maybe he's home."

"Do you want me to come with you?"

"No. It'll only take a minute. If he's there, I'll bring him out. If he isn't, we'll have to think of something else."

Jonas got out of the Bronco and took the stairway up to the second floor. Loud music blared from several of the units as he passed them. He reached Rob's apartment and knocked loudly. When there was no response, he knocked again.

"Damn," Jonas muttered. "The one time I need him, and he decides to go out."

The door of the neighboring apartment opened, and a short freckle-faced girl who looked no older than fifteen stuck her head out.

"If you're looking for Rob, he was at a party tonight. Left with some girl. The way he was grinning, I wouldn't expect him home tonight. You a friend?"

"Yeah. Friend of the family. Jonas Uhrig."

"You're Jonas? He said you helped him get out of the mess he got himself into last year, but he never said you were drop-dead gorgeous."

"Guess I'm just not his type," Jonas said with a wink. "Do you know the girl's name? It's really important that I see Rob tonight."

"No, but my roomie might. I think she had some classes with her last semester. Hang on a sec." The girl disappeared back into the apartment. She reemerged minutes later with a scrap of paper. "Her name is Liv. Weird chick. Purple hair. Tattoos. Here's her address."

Jonas took the paper and thanked the girl, rushing off before she decided to engage in small talk. He took the stairs down to the parking lot and climbed into the Bronco.

"No luck?" Kate asked.

"He isn't here, but I have the address of a girl he left a party with earlier in the night."

"I don't think he'll be thanking you for breaking up a romantic evening."

"He won't be thanking anyone if he's dead."

※　　　　　※　　　　　※

Reamun sat outside the flat and waited for the woman to exit. He had broken off following Jonas and Kate so that he could be here to watch the minor drama unfold. It wouldn't be nearly as interesting as what was to come, but it would give him more of an idea of Jonas's state of mind.

It didn't take long for the woman to emerge. She seemed to sense him there across the street and she turned to look at him, eyes narrowing. For a moment, he thought she might approach him, but instead she turned and got into to her car, driving away with a squeal of tires.

He knew she was unhappy with her part in the entire affair, but he also knew that she would do whatever it took to see things were set in motion. Some sacrifices had to be made. She would do what had to be done, as they all would.

Reamun had come too far, made too many sacrifices and laid too many plans to let it all come crashing down. The lights inside the flat went out. Thunder rolled in the distance. It had begun.

※　　　　※　　　　※

Kate drove slowly down the street as Jonas checked the numbers on the buildings. Burke was silent, staring out the window. The neighborhood was nestled inside the industrial district. Several former warehouses had been converted to spacious flats in this area.

No one else was out on this cold November night. Lights shone in a few windows, smoke billowed from fireplaces, but there was no sign of movement. Jonas felt a dark foreboding grow inside him. His skin prickled. Something evil slithered through the night, though he couldn't see it. He knew only that it was near.

An image of candlelight entered his mind. Shadows moving across stone walls. He nearly missed the flat as they passed.

"There!" Jonas pointed across the street. Before she came to a complete stop at the curb, Jonas opened his door.

"Wait!"

Jonas turned, impatient. "What?"

Kate dug around in the backseat and pulled out a gun. "Burke and I are coming with you."

"What the hell is that?" Jonas asked.

"It's a Glock, Jonas. A gun. You know, 'bam bam'?"

"I know what it is. I mean why do you have it?"

"A gal can't be too careful these days. C'mon." She slipped out of the driver's seat and opened the door for Burke. The trio made their way across the street. Burke was alert, his ears pricked as he sniffed the air.

"Doesn't look like anyone is home," Jonas said, indicating the darkened windows.

"Maybe they're just shy and like to do it in the dark," Kate said with an angelic smile.

"We can hope."

The front door of the flat was slightly ajar, and Jonas knew it wasn't that simple. Kate nudged him out of the way, moving through the door gun first, swinging right and then left before proceeding further inside, Burke after her. Jonas muttered an oath and went inside after them.

The only light in the main room came from the display cases that held several artifacts. They were all Egyptian. His blood ran cold as he stared at them. The one figurine in the center, prominently displayed, was Seth. He approached it slowly, as if it might come to life before his eyes and attack given the slightest provocation.

Burke whined.

"Jonas," Kate called. She and Burke had already made her way back to the bedroom. "You better come see this."

Jonas made his way down the hall. He stood beside Kate in the doorway of the bedroom, and his eyes widened.

Candles were lit all around the room, lending the setting an ethereal glow. The walls were intricately painted with various scenes and hieroglyphs, most of which depicted figures in various sexual acts. The large curtained bed at the center of the room was shrouded in shimmering gold curtains, preventing a view of what was beyond.

The room was absolutely silent. Burke was standing beside the bed, shivering and whimpering. Filled with a sense of dread, Jonas moved toward the bed.

"Maybe we should call the police first," Kate said.

"And say what? We found the door open and we're afraid some psychotic killer that I have a tenuous psychic link with has murdered my friend? Don't think that would wash," Jonas said. He placed his hand on the curtain, drawing in a deep breath before pulling it aside.

"Oh, christ," Kate said, lifting a hand to cover her mouth.

Jonas stared into the unseeing eyes of his friend. He was lying on his back, arms and legs outstretched. His eyes were opened wide. He looked as if he were staring into some other world that only the dead could see. Blood stained the sheets between his thighs, and on his chest lay a crimson scarf. The eye of Horus seeming to stare out at whatever place Rob was seeing.

Jonas felt some voice within him cry out in rage and pain, but it seemed distant to him. He remained fixed in place, unable to move or to look away. He couldn't seem to process what he was seeing. Couldn't fathom that the body on the bed in front of him was his friend.

"Jonas," Kate gently pulled at his shoulders. "Come on. There's nothing we can do here now. We have to call the police."

Jonas reached out a hand, carefully removing the scarf from Rob's body and putting it in his pocket.

"What are you doing?" Kate asked.

"I don't know."

"You can't just mess with evidence like that."

"Just did."

"Jonas, what's going on?"

"Let's get out of here," he said. He started for the door.

"We can call the cops from my cell phone in the car."

"Fine," Jonas said.

"You aren't going to tell them about the scarf, are you?" Kate asked.

Jonas walked out the front door, leaving it open. Burke followed him, head down.

"Damnit," Kate said, hurrying to catch up with them. They were in the Bronco waiting as she opened the driver's side door. "What the hell…"

"Get in, Kate. We don't want to draw any attention." Jonas's voice was monotone. His eyes closed.

Kate got in and shut the door. "What about the scarf?"

"It won't do any good. Might even make things harder on us. Make the call, Kate."

"Fine, but when we get done with the cops, you're going to tell me what the hell is going on in that head of yours."

❧ ❧ ❧

Reamun watched Jonas and his companions exit the flat. He noted that Jonas seemed outwardly calm and controlled despite the turmoil that must be roiling within him. There were no bellows of rage, no tears of grief or regret.

Perhaps Jonas would make a far more formidable opponent for his foe than any of them had imagined. Reamun certainly hoped so.

He knew they would call the police now and that there was nothing left to do. He turned and began walking back to his car. No one noticed his passing, just as no one but the woman had noticed his coming. He was a shadow among shadows. Any that saw dark movement in the night would chalk it up to a trick of the mind.

❧ ❧ ❧

It was nearly dawn when they finally checked into the hotel. They got a two bedroom suite for safety's sake. At least that's what Jonas told himself. In truth, he simply wanted Kate close at hand. She had a calming effect on his mind, though outwardly she seemed a chaotic person. When they entered, Kate collapsed on the couch and Burke curled up next to her.

Jonas hadn't spoken since he had called Rob's parents as they left the scene. His mind was spinning with images and emotions, his thoughts jumbled. He remained silent as he poured food and water for Burke, though the dog showed no sign of hunger.

He went into the bathroom and turned on the shower as he took off his clothes. He felt again the rage inside him, but he instinctually clamped down on it. Rage would get him nowhere. He had to think.

He stepped into the shower, letting the hot water sluice over his skin. He tried to clear his mind as he lathered his hair with shampoo, massaging his scalp in an attempt to drive away the miasma of images in his mind.

Deep down, Jonas knew that Rob had never had a chance. The killer had known Jonas would come. Had known Jonas would be too late. Had meant for Jonas to find Rob just as he had. Why?

Jonas knew it was more than mere taunting. It was far too personal for that. The killer had meant to hurt him, to anger him, but Jonas also felt that there was symbolism there that he wasn't seeing. Some message in the manner of death. It had struck him as familiar and yet he could recall no time in which he had seen such a thing.

He leaned under the spray, letting the heat flow over his face and head as he scrubbed his skin in a futile attempt to wash away the tainted feeling that had crept into his marrow.

He thought of the presence he had felt earlier in the night. He had wanted to believe it was just stress and an overactive imagination, but he could still feel it inside him, demanding that Jonas set him free.

Jonas knew that this was the same voice that drove him to wander, and he wasn't sure if that was such a good thing. If he didn't remain in control of himself, if he let that raging vengeful feeling inside him loose, he wasn't sure he could control it. He wondered if this is what it felt like to be crazy, or possessed. He supposed he could be either. It wasn't encouraging.

He turned off the water and stepped out of the shower, wrapping a towel around his waist. He looked down at the pile of discarded clothing and knew he wouldn't be able to put them on again. The stench of death clung to them now. He took a plastic laundry bag from the closet and stuffed the clothes inside. He took only his phone, wallet and the scarf from his jacket pocket before depositing it in the bag as well. He stepped out of the bathroom and Kate looked up, raising an eyebrow at his attire.

"Guess we'll have to get you some clothes tomorrow," she said. "Though the towel is nice. Might start a fashion trend."

"You don't have to stay, Kate. You've done enough. This guy is dangerous and I have no idea what he's going to do next."

"Which is exactly why I'm staying," Kate said. "I'm not going to leave you and Burke alone to go off and live my life like nothing happened. I'd be looking over my shoulder every second of every day. At least if I stay, I can help. I can do something about it, or at least try."

Jonas nodded. "I'm going to bed. We should do some research on the mythology tomorrow."

"Sounds like a plan."

Jonas stood looking at her for a moment. "You're a remarkable woman, you know."

"I know," she smiled. "Go to sleep, Jonas."

🍁   🍁   🍁

I lean against the cold windowpane, looking out at the rising sun as it sends radiant filigrees of light through the wakening day. I can still taste the young man on my lips as my tongue runs across them. Though the experience had been both invigorating and pleasurable, it had lacked passion and fury. There is only one in all the histories of Earth with whom I have felt that sense of all-encompassing satiety. That satisfaction will never again be had.

My mind drifts and I think of the Other. Closing my eyes, I seek him out with my mind. When I find him, I am surprised to find him naked lying atop a bed. His eyes are closed, brow smooth in the peace of sleep. He looks so much like the Other had so long ago.

Yet the Other is not wholly himself. He resists his true being, his power, his full glory. Even in sleep, he struggles with his own fate. I know this will work to my own advantage, but I feel a pang of regret that I cannot look upon the Other one last time in his true form. He will never have the chance to become as he once was.

Once again, another presence fills my mind, pushing me away from the Other with a powerful surge of energy.

I open my eyes. Though I am growing more powerful every day, my rebirth is not yet complete. My body requires rest, and though I am reluctant to waste time, I know I will need all my strength and powers of mind for what is to come.

*   *   *

Kate woke, hearing Jonas's wordless cry from the other room. She slid out of bed and crossed the small living area to his room. Burke was sitting next to him on the bed, looking over him worriedly.

Kate rubbed Burke's head. "It's alright. I'll take care of him."

Burke looked up at her, seeming to understand. He climbed off the bed and went to stand at the door like a sentry on watch duty.

Kate sat next to him on the bed and smoothed back Jonas's hair gently as he cried out once again. His breathing was ragged and he flinched repeatedly. "Shh. It's only a dream. You're safe, Jonas."

When he flinched again, she placed a hand on his chest. With lightning speed, his hand shot out, grasping her arm painfully. His eyes opened, full of torment and rage.

Kate didn't move. "It's alright," she soothed. "It was only a dream."

Jonas seemed momentarily confused before his grip relaxed on her arm. He closed his eyes and brought his hands to his face. "Shit," he said.

Kate massaged his shoulder. "What was it?"

"I can't explain," Jonas said. "I wasn't me. I was someone else. I was struggling. There was a blinding light. Blood." Jonas drew a deep breath. "Pain. And this voice kept saying that if I'd just let go, if I gave in, the pain would stop."

Kate stretched out next to him and gathered him in her arms. Ignoring his nakedness, she closed her eyes and ran a soothing hand along his spine. Jonas leaned into her without hesitation, his arms going around her waist. It felt good. It felt *right*. He buried his face in her hair. He realized it was the first time since he met her that she didn't have it tied back, and he lifted a hand to run his fingers through the silken strands.

Kate was suddenly aware of the taut muscles of his back beneath her fingertips, the smooth warmth of his bare thighs pressing against her own. She leaned into his touch, her head moving slightly to the side, and felt his breath against her lips.

She opened her eyes, and met his gaze, seeing her own need reflected there. His hand went to the hem of her tank top, lifting it slowly, his fingers grazing lightly over her skin as his eyes remained locked with hers. She moved her arms as he lifted the fabric over her head and tossed it away.

He lowered his head, brushing his lips over hers. She felt warm, soft, and powerfully feminine. He pulled her head towards him, and as their mouths melded he felt a jolt of fire course through him. The taste of her mouth was sweeter than he imagined. Ambrosia.

He kissed her chin, her cheek, her eyelids. He moved his hand to her breast, teasing the nipple with the rough pad of his thumb.

Kate arched her back and ran her hands over the taut muscles of his arms as he dipped his head and caught her nipple between his teeth. She sucked in a gasping breath. He moved a hand down to the gentle slope of her abdomen, pressing lightly as he drew the stiff tip of her breast more hungrily into his mouth. She moaned, her hands going to his hair, running through the soft ebony strands.

His hand moved lower to the soft down of hair at the apex of her thighs. She cried his name on a sharp intake of breath as he slipped one finger between the folds of flesh. He felt the liquid heat as he traced her skin. Her entire body was taut with need, and when he finally slipped his finger into her she cried out, lifting her hips.

Jonas slid his finger in and out as she moved against him in a ritualistic rhythm. His lips trailed down her torso until he at last tasted the sweetness of her wet silken flesh. He took the small nub between his teeth and sucked rhythmically as his finger moved within her.

Kate's whole body pulsed with awareness. She gripped his hair between her fingers, calling his name as her head flung back on the pillow. She felt a pressure rising within her to almost unbearable limits. She clung to him fiercely, her thighs pressing into his shoulders, and when he slid a second finger inside her, her body shook with convulsive shudders.

She pulled at him wildly and in a moment he was over her, swallowing her scream of pleasure with a devouring kiss. He slid into her even as her body still quaked with her climax. She wrapped her legs around his waist, meeting each swift thrust with her own movements of urgency and need.

He felt the tendrils of heat coiling tightly in his belly and moved swifter still. Again and again he thrust into her, the feel of her surrounding him filling him with unrivaled euphoria. At last his release jolted through him, and he shuddered with the violence of his release.

Kate threaded her hands soothingly through his hair, over his neck, down his back and he relaxed on top of her, nuzzling her neck. They lay like that for a long time, basking in the lingering sensations of the moment.

After awhile, he rolled off her and she felt suddenly cold. He lay on his side looking down at her with a soft smile playing on his lips, his eyes alight. She scooted against him, pulling the blanket over them. She wrapped her arms around him and placed her lips on his neck. "Sleep," she whispered against his skin. He relaxed against her, feeling as if he had finally found his place in the world. Holding her tightly, he soon drifted off into dreamless slumber.

CHAPTER 11

Jonas woke to the feel of a rough tongue running across his cheek. He squinted at the sunlight streaming through the window and looked up at Burke who was grinning at him.

"Very funny, fur face," he said as he wiped his cheek with the edge of the sheet. "Where's Kate?"

Chuff.

"Well, that certainly narrows it down," Jonas said. "Did I scare her off?"

Burke rolled his eyes and hopped off the bed.

"Well, that's a relief. Had breakfast yet?"

Chuff.

Jonas looked at the clock. It was nearly ten. "Looks like Kate took care of things while I slept in like a lazy bastard."

Chuff.

"Nobody likes a smartass dog," Jonas said as he climbed out of bed.

Burke sniffed reproachfully, looking at Jonas with mock disdain.

"Truce?" Jonas asked with a grin.

Burke grinned back, panting.

"Good, because I have work to do and the last thing I need is a pouting dog moping around. Jonas pulled the sheet off the bed and wrapped it around his waist. The hotel wasn't one that offered bathrobes to the guests, and he wasn't about to put on the clothes he had worn the last two days.

He went into the living area and picked up his phone, dialing Raiden's cell number.

"About time you called," Raiden said.

"I've been busy."

"Where are you?"

"Massachusetts," Jonas said. "Rob Woo is dead. Murdered."

"What the hell?"

"I don't know, Raiden. You need to be careful though. I think it's the same guy that hurt Bell. It's a damn long story. One I'll tell you over a beer some day, but right now I don't have the time. Just be careful. Don't go anywhere alone and try not to sleep with any strange women."

"Depends on your definition of strange," Raiden laughed.

"This is serious," Jonas said.

"Yes, mother. I'll be careful."

"Have you checked on Bell?"

"Yep. Just looked in on her actually. She looks better. Not great, but better. Her vital signs are all stable. They expect her to wake up any time. You need anything?"

"No, but thanks. I'll let you know."

After hanging up, Jonas pulled the laptop from its case, plugging it into the outlet and hooking up the phone line. When the computer connected to the internet, he started his search on Egyptian mythology. The answers lay somewhere within the stories of Horus and Seth. It was just a matter of finding them.

Kate walked in just as Jonas's phone began to ring. "I'll get it," she said, tossing him several bags with various department store labels on them.

He peeked inside, almost afraid to look at what she had picked out for him, and was relieved to see that everything seemed to be the right size and fairly standard. Two pairs of jeans, a pair of khakis, a package of T-shirts, one long sleeved dress shirt, three sweaters, jogging pants, a sweatshirt, and a package of boxer briefs. The last had him raising his eyebrow and he waved them at her as she picked up the phone. She covered the mouthpiece.

"The whole boxers or briefs question came up and I decided to sidestep it. Besides, I think they're sexy," she said with a wink. She uncovered the mouthpiece and headed into the bedroom. "Hello?"

"Well, that settles that," Jonas said to Burke.

Burke panted, sniffing the new clothes. Evidently deciding that they held no trace of cat smell, he laid back down on the couch.

Jonas was halfway through reading the third account of the battle of Horus and Seth when Kate came back into the room.

"That was one of the detectives handling the case returning a call I made earlier. Autopsy showed no defensive wounds, so Rob never tried to fight whoever it was. They found trace amounts of a hallucinogenic in his system, but it wasn't enough to kill him. The official cause of death was heart failure."

"Heart failure?" Jonas asked. "From what? He was twenty-five for chissake. He had no history of health problems."

"There doesn't seem to be any explanation for why his heart stopped. It just did. They still haven't been able to locate the girl he was with."

"What else?" Jonas asked. He could see that she was hesitating to tell him everything. As much as he didn't want to hear any of it, he knew that to figure out what was happening, he had to have all the facts.

Kate sighed. "Well, there were no signs of struggle at the crime scene. He wasn't bound in any way. The hallucinogens may have been just enough to keep him from understanding what was happening. He was sodomized, obviously. Both his semen and the semen of the attacker were found on the sheets mixed with Rob's blood. The blood came from tearing during the sodomy, though there were no other signs of violence. Interestingly enough, the attacker's semen had no sperm whatsoever."

"None?"

"Nada. Zip. Zero. Not a single swimmer in the pond."

"He's a eunuch?" Jonas asked, his sense of dread growing.

"Possibly. It isn't unheard of for eunuchs to be able to function sexually. It just takes more to get them going."

"I just did some reading. Want to know who else was a eunuch?"

"Who?"

"Seth. Apparently Horus hacked off his balls in a fit of rage," Jonas said with a wince.

"Ouch."

"Yeah."

"Coincidence?" Kate asked.

"We're traveling into freaky territory with questions like that."

"Freaky is my specialty," Kate said.

※　　　※　　　※

Reamun was still lying in bed when the doorknob to his hotel room began to turn. He looked at it curiously. After a moment, it ceased only to be flung open a second later. Liv stepped into the room and closed the door, securing the deadbolt.

She stood glaring at him, nostrils flared slightly. He noted her hair was now raven black.

"Good morning," he said as he rose from the bed, seemingly unbothered by her entrance.

"You said he would only have to be watched. That we just needed information from him. Why did you have to kill him? He was a good person."

"Did you not comfort him? Did you not council him on his path? He is well cared for."

"He is dead!" she growled.

"So he is," Reamun nodded. "It was not such a terrible death, however. In fact, I should think it was quite a pleasant one."

"All this death, all this deceit for what?"

"You know the answer."

"There has to be another way."

"You know there can be no other way. You knew what would happen when you left last night. I saw it in your eyes," Reamun said.

"I had no choice. You know that."

"And neither do I."

"You could stop this!"

"And leave us all adrift once again? Or worse, leave Uhrig to his own devices and end up dead? If he does not win this, then we're all going to suffer. You know I cannot let that happen. It must be finished. Here. Now. It is almost done."

"Many will die before it is finished. It is wrong."

"There are always casualties in war, and this war is one of utmost importance. In the end, we will all benefit from what will come."

"Not all of us," Liv said.

CHAPTER 12

Jonas stepped out of the bedroom, feeling better after putting on clean clothes. Kate looked up at him from the couch where she had been doing more research.

"What'd you find out?" he asked as he sat next to her.

"There seem to be several key figures in the myth. We start with Osiris, his sister-consort Isis, their son Horus, and their brother Seth. Seth's wife Nephthys sleeps with Osiris. Seth is understandably upset."

"Indeed," Jonas said.

"So he plots to kill Osiris," Kate said.

"Can't blame him, really."

"So Seth kills his brother and then Horus vows to avenge his father."

"Also understandable. Guy kills your dad, you can't just let that go. Lots of anger issues in that family."

"Tons. Anyway, there are many battles between the two. In one, Horus and Seth are battling in the river. Isis becomes upset, and throws her spear, accidentally hitting her son."

"Oops."

"And he begs her to let him go and she does. So then she throws it again, and it pierces Seth. And Seth gives her this sweet talk about how he's her brother, and how could she betray him so? Well, she lets him go."

"Women are so fickle," Jonas teased.

Kate rolled her eyes. "So then Horus is enraged because he could have won the battle if she hadn't let him go, so he jumps out of the river and hacks off her head."

"Ouch."

"But she gets a new one."

"Convenient," Jonas said.

"Very. Then Re, the god of the sun, told them both to chill out. He had grown tired of their endless battles. So they agree, and Seth invites Horus to stay at his palace."

"Just like that?"

"It gets even better," Kate smiled. "They're lovers."

"Lovers? First they want to kill each other and then they're humping like bunnies?" Jonas asked.

"Must've been all that tension," Kate said. "However, it looks as though they've been lovers since the beginning. There are several stories and allusions to their relationship being that of lovers. It isn't quite clear because a great deal of the pieces of the stories are missing.

"Love and war. So then what happens?"

"They have a son," Kate said.

"And that's possible how?"

"It's a myth. Play along."

"Ah," Jonas nodded, attempting to play along. "Okay, Seth and Horus have a son."

"Named Djeheuty. The Greeks called him Thoth. He was always playing peacemaker between his fathers."

"Gotta be tough when your fathers are at war with each other," Jonas said. "Wasn't he the one that replaced Horus's eye after Seth ripped it out?"

"The very same," Kate said. "But this is interesting. Not everyone agrees that Seth ripped out his eye nor that Horus ripped off his testicles. Not in any sort of battle. Apparently, it could have come about in the context of a sexual act."

"How do you lose an eye during sex? I mean, didn't his mother tell him to watch where he put that thing or he might poke an eye out?"

"Apparently not."

"And I'm not even going to get into the testicles thing."

"Sensitive issue?" Kate winked.

"You have no idea. What next?"

"This is where we have all sorts of endings to the tale, but I think the one we're dealing with is the one in which there was no clear victor, and so the battle goes on."

"What happened to the love?"

"Guess they decided they weren't right for each other or they're estranged." Kate said.

"You said Seth had a wife. What about Horus?"

"Yeah. Hathor was his wife. She was often depicted with the head of a cow."

"A cow? He married a cow?" Jonas asked.

"A very sexy cow, but she doesn't figure very prominently in the battles. At least I can't find much about her."

"I still feel like we're missing something," Jonas said.

"So do I, but at least we have most of the myth down."

"And now we have to try to get a step ahead of him."

Jonas's phone rang and he reached for it. "Uhrig."

"Mr. Jonas Uhrig?"

"Yes."

"This is Sue at MCV. You had left a request to be notified when Belladonna woke up."

"She's awake?"

"Yes, sir. She's in a lot of pain, but she's asking to see you."

Jonas breathed a sigh of relief. "So she's really going to be alright?"

"Yes. Looks like she'll be just fine. She's already making plans for her plastic surgery, even though it will be awhile before she can have it done. The wounds will have to heal first."

"Tell her I'll be there in the morning."

Jonas hung up the phone, feeling almost exuberant. It was the first good news he'd gotten in days.

"I'm going to Richmond. Bell is awake. I want to see how she's doing and if she remembers anything."

Chuff.

"I wouldn't dream of leaving you behind," Jonas winked. "But we'll have to take a plane."

Whine.

"I'm coming as well," Kate said.

"Of course. Wouldn't want to let you out of my sight. You might be abducted by aliens or something. I'll make the reservations and call a friend to pick us up at the airport."

❦   ❦   ❦

They arrived at RIC late that night, and Jonas was eerily reminded of the last time he had come home. Raiden was there to pick them up. He greeted Jonas with a bear hug and studied his eyes for a long moment before he suavely bowed before Kate.

"It is a pleasure to meet such a beautiful woman," Raiden said.

"Wow. Jonas told me you were a lady killer, but neglected to mention charm and manners."

"He would," Raiden said, winking at Jonas. "He's jealous, you see."

"Hardly," Jonas said. "But I'll let you dream."

They collected Burke and piled into Raiden's car. The night was cold and Jonas felt it in his bones. Even when Raiden turned on the heater, the chill remained.

"Maybe we should just get a hotel instead of going to my place. The guy knows where I live," Jonas said.

"I'd offer to let you stay with me," Raiden said as he flashed a grin. "But I'm expecting company."

"Surprise surprise," Jonas muttered.

"I doubt that it would make much difference," Kate said. "Besides, that's what he'd expect you to do."

"She's got a point," Raiden said.

"So we should prance boldly into danger just to thumb our noses at him?"

Chuff.

"Sure, take her side," Jonas said.

Chuff.

"Alright, we'll go home. I hope you don't mind a crowd because we only have the one bed left and no couch to turn to in case of sudden feelings of prudishness," Jonas said.

"I never get those, but I'm sure I can coax you out of any prudishness that may arise," Kate smiled.

"I'll bet."

"Do you have a sister?" Raiden asked.

"Nope," she said. "I'm an only child."

"Figures. There aren't enough women like you in the world."

❦ ❦ ❦

When they pulled up in front of the house, Jonas looked at the darkened windows and felt a pang of sadness that Belladonna wasn't there to greet them. He got out of the car, retrieved the bags from the trunk, and let Burke out.

"See you later," Raiden said. "I have a blonde and a bottle of Dom Perignon calling my name. Call if you need anything."

"Will do," Jonas said. "Stay safe."

"You too."

Raiden drove off and Jonas went to the front door. Kate followed him up the steps and Jonas noted that Burke followed as well. His normal routine of bounding headlong up the steps was gone.

As they stepped into the foyer, Jonas turned on the lights. The sight of the nearly empty living room still came as a shock.

"It's a lovely house," Kate said.

"It's an empty house."

"No, it isn't. You may have lost some furnishings and paintings, but the atmosphere is still here."

"Feels vacant," Jonas said as he looked around.

Kate glowered at him and then turned back to survey the room. "Over there," Kate pointed at the section of wall beneath the balustrade that wound up to the second floor.

"It's a wall."

"No it isn't," Kate said, taking his hand and dragging him over. "See?" She pointed at the little markings on the wall.

His parents had religiously measured him every year until he was 16, and each tiny mark represented his growth over those first 16 years of his life.

"Wow, you were a really tall kid." Kate ran her fingers over the mark that was dated 1972. He had been five years old.

"When I was a kid, Dad used to say it was the goulash Mom always cooked that made me tall. When I was eight, kids started teasing me about my height and I refused to eat it. Didn't help."

Kate smiled.

"Okay," Jonas conceded. "I see your point."

"That's refreshing," she said. "I'm going to take a shower."

"I recommend the master bath. The shower in there is the stuff of dreams. I'll take the bags up."

Jonas went into the kitchen and left Burke food and water before going upstairs with the bags. Burke, having found his appetite again, stayed behind to eat.

Jonas could hear the fall of water in the shower on the other side of the wall. Images of the night before filled his head. It still didn't feel quite real to him. She had been gone when he woke, so the realism that usually came with the morning after hadn't been there. If it weren't for his extremely vivid memories of the night, he might have thought it had all been a dream.

He put the bags on the floor of the guest bedroom, the only room that had remained fairly intact during the break-in, and opened the closet. He undressed and then put on the pair of jogging pants. He was reaching for a T-shirt when he heard a loud series of thumps from the bathroom. It sounded like she had fallen.

He ran into the master bedroom. Burke was already at the door, pawing at the knob. Jonas knocked on the door. "You okay in there?"

There was no answer.

"Kate?"

He heard a gasping sound. He tried the doorknob, expecting it to be locked, but it wasn't. He flung open the door and looked at the shower stall. Kate was sitting on the floor, huddled in the corner. Her arms were wrapped around her chest and she was staring at the floor of the stall.

She looked so small and pale and infinitely delicate to him in that moment. As if she could break into a thousand tiny pieces at the merest touch. For the first time he saw how vulnerable she truly was and it terrified him.

"Kate?" Jonas moved forward. He didn't see any obvious injuries, but that didn't mean anything. If she had fallen, she could have hit her head.

He opened the door and knelt down beside her, ignoring the spray of warm water that rushed over him. "Kate? Talk to me. What happened?"

She met his eyes then as if she had only just realized he was there. She looked haunted. He ran a hand over her hair. "Kate, I need you to tell me what's wrong."

"Nothing. I'm fine. I just slipped," she said.

"Damnit, don't lie to me. You're shaking."

She looked deep into his eyes as if she were searching his soul. "I'm okay." She tried to stand, but Jonas held her firmly by the shoulders.

"Tell me what happened. Stop holding back. You've been doing it for days and I need to know what's going on."

"It's just the stress. I'm just tired and strung out."

"Bullshit."

"Alright. Let me just finish my shower first. Please."

"So you have time to make something up?" Jonas asked.

"No. I need time to figure out how to say it and my hair needs washing. Might as well do both."

"Fine," Jonas stood and helped her up but he didn't leave.

"You're soaked," she said, indicating his jogging pants.

"Yes I am. Turn around."

"Why?"

"I'm going to wash your hair. I'm not leaving your side until I know you're okay."

"I'm okay…"

"But I don't know that because you haven't told me what's going on. So just turn around."

She did as she was told, figuring it was easier to concede this small thing than to keep staring into those dark eyes filled with worry and anger.

🍁   🍁   🍁

I stand at the end of the bed, staring down at the sleeping figure, listening to the soft rhythmic beep of the monitor nearby. Only moments ago I had attempted to reach out to the Other and was surprised when I had found the woman instead. Only she was no mere woman.

Unlike the Other, she felt my presence clearly when I reached out to her. She also knew of the one who dwelt within her soul, though she didn't know enough to use it against me. I am certain that no one else knows who she is. I do not know how she has hidden herself, but it is a secret I will keep to myself for now. It wouldn't do to be hasty about anything.

I focus once again on the figure lying in the bed. It is time to finish the task.

※ ※ ※

They had both finished drying off and had slipped into their pajamas. Jonas stood looking down at Kate who was sitting on the bed, staring intently at her toenails. He was about to start the interrogation again when his phone rang. He grumbled something and went downstairs to retrieve it.

"Mr. Uhrig, this is Detective Hernandez."

"And it's after midnight, detective," Jonas said.

"Yes. So it is. Where are you?"

"I'm at home. Why?"

There was a pause. Jonas realized it was one of those lame attempts at trying to get him to spill something. And then he suddenly went cold.

"Is this about Bell?" Jonas asked.

"I'm in the area. I need to speak with you."

"Fine. I'll be waiting."

When he hung up, Jonas tried calling the hospital, but was told that he would have to call back later. They would give no information on Belladonna's condition. He knew then that Bell was dead. Somehow the killer had gotten to her at the hospital and had finished what he had started.

Jonas stood by the front windows while he waited for Hernandez to show up. Burke had come downstairs and now sat beside him, seeming to sense Jonas's sorrow. Jonas kneeled down and rubbed his back absentmindedly as he stared out the window. Burke laid his head on Jonas's knee and peered outside at the night beyond the bay windows.

The street was quiet save for a light breeze blowing dried leaves across the cobblestones with a soft clicking sound. When he was a boy, he used to imagine that an army of beetles was marching outside his window on the walk below.

He had made all sorts of stories up for where they were marching and why. In one such story, they had been on their way to defeat the evil Rat King who was threatening to take over their domain.

His imagination had been as active as any other child, yet he had always been careful to separate reality from fantasy in his mind, never letting the two cross, for that way lie madness. Though his parents had been loving and kind, always quick with hugs and smiles and always there to listen or offer support, he had sensed in them a fear that he might one day go crazy.

He had seen a psychologist once a year who gave him various tests and asked him about his life, his dreams, and his friends. His parents called these 'brain check-ups'. They scheduled them at the same time of year that he went to see the dentist and his physician for his routine check-ups, but he had always known that other children didn't go for these 'brain check-ups' as he did.

He was never sure why they were concerned, and they never gave voice to this preoccupation with his sanity, but he always felt it. Being keenly aware of their scrutiny, he always made sure to act as normal as possible.

After his parents' deaths, he had asked his aunt if there was a family history of madness on either side. He had been concerned about his own sanity after he had begun getting the irresistible urge to travel. She had insisted there wasn't and that every Uhrig going back to the Stone Age was as sound of mind as was possible. She had been close with Jonas's mother and swore there was never any mention of any emotional or mental malady.

Two beams of light split through the darkness beyond the windows as Detective Hernandez pulled up at the curb. Jonas opened the door as he climbed the steps and stood back so the detective could pass.

Hernandez was dressed in jeans and a sweatshirt, his hair slightly mussed as if he had just woken up. He probably had just woken up, Jonas thought. He looked tired and frustrated. Jonas closed the door and waited for the detective to speak, unable to voice the question that hung in the air like a heavy cloud.

"Someone managed to slip by all the hospital staff and into Belladonna's room tonight."

Jonas just stood staring at the detective, waiting for the inevitable. He knew Hernandez was trying to gauge his reactions, but he didn't care.

"They were in and out of the room in less than five minutes by our estimation. The nurse checked on him at 12:45 and went to get another bag of saline. When she got back, he was dead."

Burke whimpered, nuzzling Jonas's leg. Jonas could only stare numbly at the detective. He'd known it was coming, but hearing the words made it reality and not merely a feeling. Hernandez's gaze never left Jonas's face as he continued.

"His eyes were cut out. Which is damn amazing because they were intact and sitting on the table when the nurse came back. Nice and neat. After removing the eyes, the killer drove two small spikes through the orbital cavity and into the brain. One would have been enough, but apparently the murderer wanted to be thorough."

Jonas thought he was going to be sick. He fought the bile rising in his throat. "Was she conscious?" Jonas's voice was barely a whisper.

"No. According to the nurse he had been given some pretty strong pain medicine that knocked him out real good."

"No one saw anything? How is that possible?"

"No one saw a soul, though we haven't had a chance to review the security tapes. We're hoping to find something on there. We don't know yet how the perp managed to get in and out so fast. You know anyone who would do this? A lover maybe?"

"She didn't have one. She had a lot of friends, but they all loved her. Everyone did. She was an amazing human being. No one who knew her would do this, Detective. No one."

"He have anyone harassing him?"

"Not that I know of," Jonas said. "I wasn't around a whole lot. I'm not sure she would have told me if there had been. She was a very positive person. If something bad happened to her, she tended to shrug it off and look to the future. She didn't dwell on things."

"Sounds like an ideal human being," Hernandez said.

"She was."

"Someone didn't think so."

"Someone was wrong," Jonas said. He didn't have the energy to make further protestations. He felt as if his heart were literally broken. "Will you let me know if you get something more? I know you can't tell me everything, but if you get any idea of who did this, I'd like to be informed."

"We'll see how it plays out," the detective said.

Jonas wanted to strangle him, but managed to suppress the urge long enough to see the detective out the door. When he closed the door behind Hernandez, he leaned his head against it, fighting the feelings of rage, guilt, frustration, and anguish.

Whine.

"I know, pal," Jonas said, reaching out a hand to stroke Burke's head. "I know."

After a moment, Jonas reached for the phone to call Raiden. After three rings, Raiden answered, sounding slightly winded.

"This better be important," he growled. "If it wasn't your name on the Caller ID, I wouldn't be answering the phone right now."

"Bell is dead," Jonas said.

"Fuck. I'm so sorry, Jonas. How?"

"Murdered. They don't know who. He took out her eyes, Raiden."

"Fuck."

"Yeah."

"You going to tell me what's going on?" Raiden asked.

"Some sicko just seems to be targeting people I'm close to. Which means you're a prime target."

"But who? Why?"

"I don't know. It doesn't make much sense to me yet, but I'm working on it. Maybe you should take a vacation. Lay low for awhile."

"And leave you to the wolf? I don't think so. I'm coming over there." Raiden said.

"No, I'm okay. He doesn't seem interested in killing me. Just people around me. That means you."

"I don't give a damn. I'm not going to let this happen to you, Jonas."

"You can't help, Raiden. Just get somewhere he can't find you. If I know you're safe, then that's one less thing for me to worry about."

"Going off to hide while you're in deep shit isn't my thing, Jonas. I don't like it."

"Neither do I, but that's the way it has to be. I'll be okay. I need to know that you're safe, though. Do this for me, Raiden."

Raiden sighed. "Alright. For now. Stay in touch, though. I'll have my cell with me. If you need anything, and I mean anything, you call me."

"Okay, but I may not call for awhile. Not until I think it's safe."

"Take care of yourself," Raiden said.

Jonas ended the call, relieved that Raiden would be out of harm's way. At least for awhile. Jonas knew that if he didn't figure this out soon, and stop what was happening, none of the people he loved would ever be truly safe.

When Jonas went back up to the bedroom, he found Kate already asleep beneath the blankets. As badly as he wanted to know what had happened earlier, he was relieved that he wouldn't have to tell her about Belladonna. He didn't think he was up for it.

He lay down in bed and stared at the ceiling. He felt like crying, screaming, violently avenging this most heinous crime. He did none of those things. He lay completely still and gazed at the ceiling until exhaustion finally overcame him.

CHAPTER 13

Near dawn, Kate woke up as she felt the bed shift. The illumination from the street lights through half open blinds provided enough light for her to see Jonas get up and walk out of the room. She waited for the hall light to come on or to hear the sound of the bathroom door close, but neither came.

When she heard the squeak of wood on the stairs, she got up. She felt the need for a drink of water herself. As she felt her way down the steps, she cursed him for not turning on any lights. Living in the same house all your life would give you the ability to walk through it blindfolded. She, however, didn't even know where the light switches were.

Downstairs, the foyer and living room were almost completely dark. She heard movement in the living room, but couldn't see well enough to distinguish one shadow from the next.

"Jonas?" she called softly.

There was no reply. She stood on the bottom step, wondering if she should just go back to bed when a soft glow emanated from the kitchen. She felt something brush against her leg and nearly jumped. Then she realized it was Burke. The dog whined and stared up at her before going to sit at the door to the kitchen.

He looked inside and then back at Kate as if beckoning her to follow. Kate followed the light, managing not to bump into anything on her way across the living room.

When she stepped into the kitchen, she saw Jonas seated at the table in front of the laptop. She walked over to stand in front of him, but he didn't look up. Burke whined again from the doorway but didn't come into the room.

"Jonas?"

He started typing something, still not looking up or acknowledging her presence. She realized that he looked half asleep, his eyes glazed over. The sound of Jonas typing on the keyboard seemed to grow louder as she moved around the table. As if all the world held its breath. A shiver of dread went through her.

She stood behind him and looked at the computer screen. Several lines glowed on the monitor. Before she could read them, Jonas stood and began walking toward the living room.

She followed him, wanting to be sure that he made it back to bed safely from this somnambulistic journey. He walked slowly up the steps and into the bedroom. She watched as he lay down on the bed and closed his eyes.

With great care, she lifted the blanket and covered him, brushing his hair back from his face. He didn't stir. She wanted to gather him in her arms and protect him from what was happening, but she knew the only way to truly protect him was to find out what was going on.

She crept back downstairs and found Burke still waiting in the kitchen.

"He's back in bed," she said.

Chuff.

"Now let's find out what he was up to."

She turned on the light and went to the table, reading the words on the screen aloud. This she did for Burke's benefit. She had the odd feeling that he understood more of what was going on than either she or Jonas did.

I am the originator of the divine force, and I shall be born once more unto the lands of Earth in the day of the vengeance of my father. Hear me, for my voice is louder than the thunder of Seth. See me, for my visage will make the weak of heart tremble in my passing. Feel me, for my might is more powerful than any other who dwells in this realm. Know me, for I am the Avenger.

My path is before me and I shall slay the enemy and cut off his head to deliver to the god of the Sun. I shall tear apart his body and send them into the Abyss where they shall be forever lost to this realm.

Kate sat for awhile reading the passage a few more times before looking at Burke. "So should we tell him?"

Chuff.

"I'll take that as a yes, but you know how sensitive he is about these things."

Chuff.

"Okay, then you tell him. He'll think I'm delusional."

Burke raised his brows. *Whine.*

"Oh, okay," she said. "But he isn't going to like it."

CHAPTER 14

❀

Jonas woke to the smell of frying bacon. He nearly drooled as he rolled out of bed and made his way downstairs. He was halfway to the kitchen when he remembered Detective Hernandez's visit last night and that he would have tell Kate about the murder. He didn't want to think about it. He wasn't sure he could keep going under the weight of the murders of his dearest friends if he let himself stop to think about them.

"Good morning," Kate said as he walked in. "You look like hell."

He smiled despite his grim thoughts. She was standing at the sink, the morning sunlight rippling through her unbound hair. "You look delicious."

"You'll have to eat pancakes and bacon first and then if you still have room, we'll discuss desert." She placed a plate stacked high with food on the table and pointed at the chair. "Eat."

"I don't think I can, and even if I could, it would take me days to eat all that. We have to talk."

"We'll talk after you eat. No complaining." Kate got her own plate and sat down. Jonas noticed she hadn't gotten nearly as much for herself.

Jonas saw that Burke was chowing down on his own large serving of bacon and decided that he would attempt it. He sat down at the table and took a bite of pancakes. His hunger won out over his inner turmoil and in the end he ate nearly half of what Kate had given him.

"I'm stuffed. We need to talk," Jonas said.

"Okay. You first." Kate began clearing away the dishes and putting them in the sink.

"The call I got last night was from Detective Hernandez. It was about Bell."

Kate slowly turned from the sink to look at him. "Is she...?"

Jonas nodded. "He got to her. No one saw him come or go, but he got to her."

"I'm so sorry," she said. "I don't know what to say."

"I should have known. I should have done something to protect her."

"You couldn't have known and you couldn't have protected her," Kate said. "You aren't responsible for this."

"There's more," Jonas said, feeling suddenly very sick. He told her how Belladonna had been murdered. By the time he was finished, Kate was pale.

"At least she didn't feel anything."

Jonas nodded, but it was little comfort.

"We'll find him, Jonas. We'll stop him."

"I hope so," Jonas said. No longer able to discuss Belladonna's murder without risk of falling apart, he changed the subject. "Your turn. What happened last night in the shower?"

Kate sighed and stood up. "We'll get to that in a minute. You have to come see this first."

Puzzled, Jonas followed her over to the counter. She opened the laptop, and he read the words on the screen.

"It was on the table," she said. "But I moved it so we could eat first."

"He was here?" Jonas asked, anger creeping into his voice.

"No, Jonas. He wasn't here."

"How can you know that? How else would the message get there?"

"You typed it," Kate said.

He stared at her uncomprehending, as if she were speaking another language.

"You got up last night. I followed you down here. I thought you were just getting a glass of water, but when I came in, you were sitting right there at the table typing this."

"That isn't funny," Jonas warned.

"No, and it isn't meant to be. I called your name twice before I realized you weren't awake. After you were done you got up and went back to bed. It was you, Jonas. I saw it with my own eyes."

Jonas read the message again, trying to absorb what she was saying. "But I don't remember any of that. Where the hell would I come up with this stuff?"

"You were asleep," Kate said. "Of course you don't remember. I don't know where the words came from Jonas, but I know you typed them."

Jonas had a sudden flash of memory of the morning after Belladonna had been assaulted. Before leaving the house, he had put his laptop in its case and had taken it out to the car with him. It hadn't been taken or destroyed because it *hadn't been there.*

He ran a hand through his hair, still staring at the monitor. "Maybe I am crazy," he said.

"You aren't crazy," Kate said. "It's called sleepwalking."

"Somnambulism doesn't normally involve leaving yourself creepy messages," Jonas said.

"Nothing about what is happening could be labeled normal, Jonas. It's just another part of the puzzle we have to fit together."

Jonas felt as if his head were going to explode. All these tiny fragments were somehow related, but he couldn't make them fit. It was like a thousand pieces of jigsaw puzzle that were all the same color.

"It doesn't make sense," he said finally.

"It does, we just have to figure out how."

"Before he kills someone else," Jonas said.

❦   ❦   ❦

Reamun sat in his car, watching the house. He was becoming increasingly frustrated with Uhrig. The man showed no signs of evolving or reaching his true power. There was little time.

His foe, on the other hand, was nearly complete with his preparations. Unless something drastic changed, there would be no battle. It would merely be a slaughter. He couldn't let that happen.

The future depended upon Uhrig doing things the right way. Reamun had been so certain that things were progressing as planned, but now he had to doubt that it would work at all. If Uhrig's progress didn't begin to pick up pace soon, Reamun would have to intervene and force Uhrig into action. Too much was at stake to allow it all to come to ruin because the man was in denial.

However, there was still a ray of hope. Uhrig had yet left one giant stone unturned. Perhaps that would be the one that started the avalanche.

❦   ❦   ❦

The phone rang just as Jonas was about to ask Kate about the shower the night before.

"Uhrig."

"This is Detective Hernandez. I need you to come down here and look at this security video, see if you recognize anyone."

"You have the killer on tape?"

"Yeah," Hernandez said. "When can you be here?"

Jonas noted the man's tone was much less confrontational than usual. Instead of relief, he felt a sense of growing dread. "I'll have to find a ride."

"I'll send a car for you. Can you be ready in ten minutes?"

"Yeah. Ten minutes should be enough time."

"I'll see you then."

Jonas hung up and looked at Kate. "I'm going to look at the security tape from the hospital. I think you and Burke should come with me."

"I doubt they allow dogs in the police department," she said.

"I don't want to leave you here alone."

Burke padded over to sit beside Kate and looked up at Jonas quizzically.

"We'll be fine, Jonas. I have my Glock and Burke. I'll be better protected than you will."

"It isn't me that I'm worried about. He won't come after me until his little game is done."

"I think sitting in a car or out on the sidewalk would make us more like sitting ducks than being here. We'll be fine. Stop worrying."

Chuff.

Jonas hesitated. He didn't want them out of his sight, but couldn't think of any alternative. "Okay. I'll be back soon. Call me if you need anything. If Burke starts acting weird or anything else happens…"

"We'll stay right here and stare at the walls until you get back," Kate smiled.

"Right. Can you handle it, bud?" Jonas asked Burke.

Chuff. Burke licked his hand.

Jonas stood, hesitating before going up to get dressed.

"You told the detective ten minutes," Kate reminded him. "You'd better hurry."

Jonas nodded and went upstairs. He dressed quickly and as he came back down, he heard a knock on the door. Kate waved at him as he passed through the living room and he had to force himself not to repeat his safety warnings. He smiled and opened the door, greeting the uniformed officer who seemed less than happy at playing chauffer.

Jonas checked the street as he made his way out to the squad car behind the officer, but saw no sign of anything amiss. There were a few people walking down the sidewalk. Cars passed every few seconds along the street. A few people were out raking leaves. It seemed to be just like any other November day. Only it wasn't just any November day. Nothing about the past week had been normal.

Jonas knew that he couldn't trust the façade of peace and tranquility. Though he saw nothing out of the ordinary, he had no idea what he should be looking for. He could be looking straight at the killer and not know it.

He climbed into the cruiser and buckled his seatbelt, still staring down the block as if he expected some three headed dragon to suddenly appear and begin scorching houses with its flaming breath. When they pulled away from the curb and started down the street, Jonas fought the urge to look back. He was paranoid, but he had reason to be. However, he couldn't let his agitation become obvious to the cop.

Neither he nor the cop spoke the whole way to the station. The beeps and intermittent voices over the police radio provided enough background noise to forgo the necessity of idle chatter. Jonas was relieved. He wasn't sure he could have passed the small talk test.

When they pulled up in front of the station, Hernandez was waiting outside.

"You don't look like you slept," Hernandez observed as Jonas climbed out of the car.

"Neither do you," Jonas said.

Hernandez smiled the first genuine smile Jonas had ever seen on his face. "I guess it comes with the territory. I have the tape ready."

Hernandez led Jonas back through a series of hallways to a small room where a television and VCR were set up. The detective indicated that Jonas should take a seat while he started the video tape.

"We have three shots of the guy, but none of them show his face. They match with the timeframe of the murder. I'm hoping you'll recognize something about him that will give us an idea about who this guy is."

Hernandez started the tape and Jonas saw an elevator door.

"That's the first floor. Here in a second, you'll see him get in."

Jonas watched the screen and the moment the blurred dark figure appeared at the elevator doors, he knew it was the killer. The hairs stood up on the nape of his neck. The man had short dark hair, but the video was in black and white, so it was impossible to tell the exact color. He wore a dark sweater, jeans, and moved with the grace of a panther.

Jonas knew immediately why the detective no longer seemed suspicious of him. Though the figure on the screen was little more than a dark blur, the build was different. Not only was the hair short, compared to Jonas's shoulder length locks, but the shape of the face was thinner, the outline of the nose more aquiline than Jonas's.

Something about him kindled some memory deep in Jonas's mind, but he couldn't seem to bring it to the fore.

"Anything?" Hernandez asked.

"No, sorry," Jonas lied.

"Here's the next one. Here he's just getting off the elevator onto the ICU floor."

Jonas watched as the elevator doors opened. As before, the figure seemed impossibly darker than his surroundings. As if shadows of his own making obscured his features. The camera should have caught him clearly. The light was bright in both the hallway and the elevator. He had gone the same way himself. And yet even though the killer seemed to look directly into the camera as he passed, nothing more than blackness upon the clear backdrop of the hospital corridor was viewable.

"I can't recognize anything. It's too dark," Jonas said.

"Just keep your mind clear and concentrate on the way he moves. Maybe it'll spark a memory," detective Hernandez said. "The last clip is of him entering the stairwell. It leads out into the parking lot and he wasn't caught on any other cameras."

Jonas watched, almost wishing he could look away. The tenebrous figure slithered into view and then paused. It seemed to Jonas that this was not a human at all, but some strange and alien creature with powers of dark magic that walked the Earth with the shape of a man and the soul of something far more wicked. It turned then, looking directly at the camera, and though its features were completely enveloped in blackness, it seemed to be staring directly at him. Jonas felt as if he were looking into the abyss. He shook as the feeling of something cold and foul slithered into his veins. It pervaded his entire being.

He wanted to scream, to turn away, to shout some warning about the terrible *thing* that was living among them. Disguised as human but *not* human. It was something far worse than any mere Bundy or Manson. This was a force so inexplicably evil and terrifying that it could only be felt by that primordial instinct that everyone had, but few people listened to anymore.

Hernandez spoke then, but it seemed to Jonas that he was speaking from the bottom of a great pool. His voice was muffled until only the tone could be discerned. That tone was so natural, so devoid of emotion that Jonas wanted to grab him and shake him by the shoulders. Couldn't he *see*? Didn't he *know*? How could he be so blind to what he had just witnessed on that video tape?

Jonas tried to speak, but realized that he wasn't breathing. He couldn't seem to draw air into his lungs. He felt as if he were suddenly drowning in that same oozing evil that chilled his bones.

Hernandez was speaking more urgently now, hovering over Jonas with a look of concern creasing his brow. He grabbed Jonas's shoulder and crouched down in front of his chair. Jonas couldn't move. He couldn't form the words that ran through his mind. He couldn't breathe. His vision began to blur into darkness.

※ ※ ※

He is afraid. I feel his terror as if it were my own. I am so close to him that I am nearly inside him. I can hear his heartbeat in my ears, feel the cold shivers that cause him to shake, I can feel his breath trapped in his chest. This is as close as I have been to him in a very long time.

There had been a time when I had been this close with the Other, but in a way that had been much different. Those were easier times. Times when we were not enemies. There had been no fear then, no hatred, no discontent. We were almost as one. We would have reached that singularity if we had been left unhindered.

Yet they feared our power. They feared that they would no longer have any use in this realm if we were allowed to follow the path we were meant to take. And so we were torn apart most cruelly, and it is the pain of that most grievous act that brings us to this place.

I am not joyful at his suffering now. For the first time I believe he feels what it is that I felt and have carried inside me since that dis-union long ago. He knows the pain now. He can no longer hide behind his fury and his wrath. I am moved to pity for him. I care for him still.

Yet I cannot let these feelings stop me from what must now be done. Our paths, which once led us along the same road, have again converged. Only this time there will be but one of us that reaches the other side of the mountain that lies in our way.

It is not my choice to have it be so. It is beyond my power to stop the cycle we have been thrown into. It is as it must be.

I reach out to free him from his waking nightmare. A gentle caress in his mind to soothe him. To erase the terror he feels, but not the pain. I want him to remember that pain for the rest of his days as I remember my own.

He stills. I can feel his confusion at the mix of emotions he feels. He does not know me and yet he does. He feels me there and yet denies it to himself. He is full of conflict and paradox.

He lingers there for a moment on the precipice of fear, doubt, anger, and indecision. He wants so badly to reach out, to know me and what it is that I desire from him that he seems almost as a child to me.

And then he is free, broken away from the bonds that held him. I feel his breath rush into his lungs and then he is gone from me, his walls once more erected carefully around him. I will break them down again later.

❦ ❦ ❦

Suddenly, Jonas could breathe again. He sucked in great lungfuls of air as Detective Hernandez asked him if he was alright.

"Fine," Jonas wheezed.

"You don't look fine."

"It was just…the shock. I don't know. Seeing the killer. It's just a bit much right now. I thought I could handle it."

"No need to explain," Hernandez said. "You haven't had any time to let it all sink in. I wouldn't have had you come down here if it wasn't so important that we get this guy. Most people would have cracked after the second tape."

"That's comforting."

"Are you sure you don't recognize anything about him?"

"I'm sure," Jonas said. He hoped he sounded more confident than he felt.

"Nothing in the way he moved or carried himself?"

"No," Jonas said.

"Will you let me know if you remember anything?"

"Yeah. Sure."

"I guess you're going to be at the funeral?"

"Funeral?" Jonas asked. He hadn't even thought about it.

"Some of his friends are taking care of it. I expect it'll be Thursday."

"I never liked funerals," Jonas said. "Never saw the point."

"You don't want to pay your last respects?"

"She's dead, Detective. It really wouldn't offend her. I have no wish to stand around in some morbid ritual watching the sorrow of others when my own is enough to keep me awake."

Hernandez nodded, seeming satisfied. "Some people need that. Some people don't."

Jonas remained silent. He didn't know what else to say.

"I'll have one of the boys drive you home."

"Thank you."

Hernandez left the room and Jonas relaxed back into his chair. He was exhausted. Whatever it had been that had gripped him a few minutes earlier couldn't have been the product of his own imaginings. Unless he was going insane. He almost wished it were as simple as that.

"You Uhrig?" a cop asked from the doorway.

"Yeah."

"Come on. I'll give you lift. I'm Officer Kern."

"Thanks."

Jonas followed him out to the squad car. Unfortunately, this officer was feeling chatty.

"Beautiful day."

"I guess it is," Jonas said.

"Sunshine. Fifty degrees. And I don't have to be back at work for two days. Perfect."

Jonas buckled his seatbelt and nodded, unable to make small talk.

"You got a family?"

"No," Jonas said.

"You should. It's the best. I got a wife and four kids. Number five on the way."

"Congratulations."

"Thanks," Kern said and smiled a genuine smile. "Nothing like coming home to family. Little kids are so happy to see you whenever you get home. You can go to the store for ten minutes and you come back and they're all over you smiling those huge smiles."

"Sounds nice."

"Oh, it's better than nice. It's heaven. And the wife. She's my angel. You ever been in love?"

Jonas hadn't, but he thought that perhaps the chance was there with Kate. If they lived long enough. "No."

"You're missing out. It's out there, man. You just gotta want it. You gotta leave yourself open to it. A lot of guys, they're afraid or they think it's going to cramp their style. They don't know what they're missing. True love, man. Soul mates."

They pulled up in front of Jonas's house and the officer pulled to the curb. "I'll keep it in mind. Thanks for the lift."

"No problem. Have a good one."

As Jonas walked up the steps, the officer's words lingered in his mind. Something in what he'd said had struck a chord in him. Not about the wife and kids, but about love. The idea of soul mates resonated deep within him and he couldn't figure out why. He had never believed in such things. Yet it seemed important.

CHAPTER 15

"You look like hell," Kate said when Jonas stepped into the foyer. He was pale, his lips drawn into a thin line. "What happened?"

"Couldn't see anything on the tape. Just shadows."

"And?"

Jonas shook his head. "It was just creepy."

"You didn't recognize him?"

"There wasn't really anything to see. I felt like something was familiar, but I couldn't put my finger on it. I don't know. It's all jumbled in my head. I can't think."

Burke rubbed against his legs and Jonas reached down to pet him.

"Who else will this guy target?" she asked.

"The only ones left are my Aunt Millie, Raiden, Burke, and you. Unless we start counting casual acquaintances. I know many people. I'm just not close with most of them. Moving around so much hasn't left me with a great deal of close relationships. I already told Raiden to take a long vacation and stay low-profile."

"Where's your Aunt Millie?"

"Georgia. She lives outside Atlanta." Jonas reached for his cell phone, but didn't dial. "What the hell am I going to say? She can't just up and leave. She hates to travel."

"Does anyone live with her?"

"She has a live-in housekeeper and a part time driver."

"Neighbors?"

"No one near. She lives on a sizeable plantation. There are gardeners and such that come and go on a regular basis during the weekdays, but no one there other than Greta nights and weekends."

"Just call her Jonas," Kate said. "Tell her the truth, or as much of it as you can."

Jonas stared at the phone, and then finally dialed.

"Huhlo?"

"Greta, it's Jonas."

"Jonas! Your aunt has been very worried about you. You know that she heard about your house? About Belladonna? She tried to call you, but you don't answer your phone."

Jonas smothered a curse. He had forgotten to give his aunt his new cell phone number when he had switched companies. "I'm sorry, Greta. I should have called sooner. Can I speak with her?"

"She's taking her nap, but I'll see if I can wake her. You should visit more often you know. She is an old woman. She has no one else. She has been overwrought with worry these past few days."

"I know," Jonas said. The idea of his steadfast aunt overwrought was one he couldn't picture.

After a lengthy pause, Millie picked up the phone and she didn't sound at all fragile or overwrought. She sounded pissed. "Jonas Uhrig, you get down to Georgia right this instant."

"Millie, I have to…"

"No, Jonas. No excuses this time. You're in deep trouble. I told your parents they should have explained everything to you when you were a boy, but they insisted it would be best you didn't know. They thought it was all just a fairy tale. Well, they were wrong."

"What are you talking about?" Jonas asked.

"Your destiny, Jonas. Come to Georgia. I'll have Greta get your room ready."

Jonas gripped the phone tighter, trying to figure out what she meant. "Millie, why can't you just explain it to me now?"

"Don't argue with me, boy. Are you bringing the dog?"
"Of course," he said. "And a friend."
"Lady friend?" she asked with keen interest.
"Yes," Jonas said.
"One bedroom or two?"
Jonas glanced at Kate, "Two."
"That's a good sign. At least she isn't a trollop like the last few girls you…"
"I think that's enough. We'll be there on the next flight. This better be good."
"Oh, it isn't good at all, my dear boy. Not at all."

❦ ❦ ❦

They arrived in Atlanta early that evening. Millie had sent her driver to pick them up. Gregor was a very tall, very gaunt man who always reminded Jonas of Lurch from the Addams Family. He couldn't recall ever seeing the man smile, and he had only heard him speak a dozen times in all these years. Gregor had been employed as Millie's driver for all of Jonas's life, and possibly many years before that.

Gregor remained silent in the front of the limo as he drove them out of town and toward the plantation. For awhile, Kate and Jonas remained silent as well, watching the scenery through the windows.

"How far is it?" Kate asked.

"We should be there in about twenty minutes. Not long. Fallwood is a relatively small town. My aunt is something of a celebrity there. It's mostly farms and middle class people and her estate is like the castle of the kingdom," Jonas said as he stroked Burke's head.

"Are the two of you close?"

"Yeah. In an odd way," Jonas said. "She's always worried over me, but not in that mother hen way. Maybe 'kept an eye on' is a better way of putting it. I haven't been out to see her in a long time. A few years. Every time I thought to come, I had to be someplace else."

"But she has obviously known what you were up to."

"Yeah, I guess she has. She and my father were very close growing up and she never had children of her own."

"Why not?"

"My uncle was gone a great deal of the time. He was an archaeologist, but Millie seemed content with it. She always said that their separations made their time together more special. However, she refused to raise a child alone and my uncle couldn't stay put long enough to help."

They pulled through the gates of the property and made their way down a long winding path. When at last the house came into view, Kate gaped.

"It's a freakin' mansion."

"It's a monstrosity," Jonas said. "All that house just for her and her housekeeper. Her husband died when I was little. Some sort of cave-in. When he died though, she was in mourning for years and I remember my father trying to persuade her to move to Virginia to be with us, but she wouldn't have it. She refuses to give it up. It's been in the family for over two hundred and fifty years."

"It didn't go to your father?"

"No. He didn't want it. He always preferred smaller more cozy places I suppose. He gladly let Millie have it."

Greta stood on the porch waiting as Gregor stopped the car and went around to open their doors and get their bags. She was a hefty woman, though not excessively fat. She looked sturdy and solid, as if she could withstand just about anything. Burke bounded up the steps and sat in front of Greta, panting happily.

"Why, Mr. Burke!" Greta smiled warmly at the dog. "I think you've grown. You're still too skinny. I have some special treats for you in the kitchen. And you," she said as Jonas ascended the steps with Kate. "You're both too skinny as well. I'll fix that. Come along. Millie is waiting in the drawing room.

Kate looked at Jonas. She mouthed the words "drawing room" at him with an incredulous stare. Jonas grinned and shook his head, motioning Kate inside.

Kate marveled at the richness of the house as Greta led them inside. The marble floor shone brightly with the reflections of the hand made lamps that lined the entryway. The walls were painted with an elaborate mural of Christ's crucifixion. Blood flowed from angry wounds. Jesus' face was contorted in agony. She thought it a very odd way to greet guests. She looked at Jonas.

"Millie had that done when I was a kid," he said.

"It's creepy."

"Her idea of a joke to scare away unwelcome visitors. We're agnostic. Kinda grows on you after awhile."

"I see where you get your sense of humor," Kate said.

In the drawing room, Millie sat in a large wing backed chair covered in soft brocade. She was a small woman with grey hair shot through with strands of gold and pale blue eyes. Despite her diminutive size, she seemed almost regal in her posture. Her face was nearly unlined. She looked nowhere near a woman in her seventies. She had either a really good plastic surgeon or really good genes.

Her gaze was sharp and full of intelligence. The painting above the fireplace showed her in her younger days, blonde hair shimmering in the sun.

Kate could see no family resemblance between this woman and Jonas other than that they were both very beautiful. Millie was fair where Jonas was dark skinned with eyes the color of obsidian. Jonas was exceedingly tall where Millie was petite. Kate decided he must have gotten more than a fair share of his mother's genes rather than his father's.

Millie nodded at both Kate and Burke with a majestic smile before turning her eyes to Jonas.

"I had thought never to see you again," she sighed. "Sit. All of you. Greta, tea please."

"Of course," Greta said, bustling out of the room.

"Millie, this is Kate Barnett. She's a photographer," Jonas said.

"Pleased to meet you," Kate smiled.

"You've been helping Jonas?" Millie asked, her gaze narrowing slightly.

"Doing what I can," she said, trying not to squirm under Millie's scrutiny.

"Do you have family?"

"Not that I know of," Kate said. "My mother died a few years ago. I never knew my father."

"How did you come to know Jonas?"

"Really, Millie..." Jonas began.

Kate waved a quelling hand at him. "It's alright, Jonas." She turned to Millie. "I was at a crime scene in Cincinnati and noticed a red scarf. It reminded me of a story Jonas had written a few years back, so I called him. Things just started happening and we decided to try to figure it out together."

Millie nodded. "I know about the scarf and the assaults and murders. And what have you figured out?"

"It depends on which one of us you ask," Kate smiled. "I think that this wanderlust Jonas has had all these years that seems to be driving him to the same places where the murders occur is coming from within him. I think he's following the killer. I think he's been trying to stop it, even though he wasn't aware of it."

Millie raised an eyebrow and looked at Jonas. "And what do you think?"

"I think some psycho is following me."

"How very egotistical," Millie said. She turned back to Kate in obvious dismissal of Jonas's assessment. "Tell me what else has happened."

Kate told her about the hotel explosion, the strange messages on Jonas's computer, the research they had done, Jonas's nightmares, and the events surrounding the murders of Belladonna and Rob

Woo. As she finished, Greta came in and placed a plate of scones, cookies, and muffins on the coffee table and poured tea for everyone.

"Will there be anything else?"

"That's all, Greta. Thank you."

"Good, then. Dinner will be in half an hour." She left just as quickly as she came.

Millie took her time stirring sugar and cream into her tea.

"Why are we here, Millie?" Jonas asked. "What do you know about all this?"

Millie sighed, her expression softening a bit as she looked at him. "Your parents wanted so badly to protect you from all of this."

"How could they have known?"

"To answer that, I have to start from the beginning. You must understand that I never told you any of this before out of respect for your parents' wishes. Once it became clear that the prophecy was indeed unfolding, I couldn't contact you, though I tried."

"I understand," Jonas said. "Tell me."

"Thirty-six years ago, your uncle Henry was helping at a dig near Idfu. He didn't usually have me along on his jobs, but he became so enamored with Egypt that he begged me to come out. Well, I wasn't going alone. I hate to travel. So I asked your mother if she'd come with me, and she accepted. She had only just found out she was pregnant with you and I told her it would be her last chance for a long time to get a nice relaxing trip."

"Very sly," Jonas commented.

"I thought so," Millie said with a smile. "Anyway, we had been there for about a week when they finally uncovered the entrance to the temple. They were all very excited and Henry sent one of the students to fetch us. Said we had to come see. We got there just as they opened the door.

"There was a feeling about the place as we stepped in. Like there were eyes all around watching. It was just the five of us to go in first.

Your mother and I, Henry, Professor Sampson, one of the students, and Sampson's dog.

"They started reading the markings on the walls. Your mother and I were just looking around when the young student remarked that there was something really strange about the temple. Well, I could have told him that. It felt alive. The longer we stayed in there, the more overwhelming the feeling was.

"We were only in there about twenty minutes when the lights they had set up went out. We scrambled about for a minute trying to find our way to the entrance, but the door was closed. We couldn't get it open. The last thing I remember was that your mother screamed. I woke up two days later in the hospital."

"Jesus," Jonas said. "Mom never told me any of this. What happened?"

"We were told that the Egyptian government had shut down the site and had confiscated all the notes and photos from the team. We were all made to sign confidentiality agreements saying we wouldn't speak of what we had found there in the temple."

"You signed it?" Kate asked.

"We had to. They were very clear that we would have difficulty getting back home if we didn't. The implication was that we wouldn't be alive to make it home. Anyway, the team regrouped just before we left Egypt and they all compared what they knew about what had happened. The doctors there told us we had all suffered from the heat, but it was a cool day in January.

"The temple appeared to be much older than the temple of Horus at Idfu, they said. And the hieroglyphs made it clear that it was a sort of holding place for the spirits of the gods until the day came when Horus and Seth would once again battle, and the gods would be restored."

"So they were trapped there? All the gods and goddesses just waiting to be set free?" Kate asked.

"So they said. The writings said that those who entered would carry the spirits of the gods with them, and that through them, the gods would be reborn and the battle would start anew when they had once more reached their full power. None of us really believed any of it at the time. We went back to our lives. The Egyptian government evidently covered up any sign of the temple.

"And then, when you were born seven months later, you had a birthmark on the back of your tiny little head. It was the Eye of Horus."

Jonas's hand went to the back of his head.

"Turn around," Kate said. Jonas complied and sat silently while Kate parted his hair in the back.

"It's right in the middle there," Millie said. "Clear as day until he finally grew some hair."

"She's right," Kate whispered.

"Your parents both refused to believe. They made all sorts of excuses for the birthmark. But that isn't all. A year later when the good professor had a son, he also had a birthmark. It was a depiction of Seth."

"Shit," Jonas said.

"Watch your language, dear," Millie admonished.

"So Jonas is carrying around a god inside him?" Kate asked.

"If you believe the writings on the temple wall."

"Do you?"

"Yes," Millie said. "I do. I'm not one to be taken by flights of fancy or stories about Bigfoot, but I know when to open my eyes and see the truth. No matter how unbelievable it may seem."

From the dining hall, a light tinkling of bells announced dinner. Millie stood. "Come along. We don't want your dinner getting cold. Greta would be very upset."

Jonas, Kate, and Burke followed her into the dining hall. A long table sat in the center of the room. It was long enough to seat two dozen people. Greta had laid out place settings at one end. There was a large plate on the floor for Burke, filled with several different kinds of meat, all sliced thin and piled high.

As they sat down, Kate suddenly stiffened. "Wait a minute. You said Professor Sampson's dog was there. What happened to it?"

"We never found her. They said she ran off when they finally opened the door to get us out," Millie said.

Everyone looked at Burke, who was intent on his plate.

"This is ridiculous," Jonas said.

"Hardly," Millie said as Greta started serving the meal. "I've thought your Burke was probably one of the carriers ever since he showed up on your doorstep."

"My dog is a god?" he asked, quirking an eyebrow. "That's a bit much to swallow."

"No, he's merely a carrier. He's still very much a dog. As you are very much yourself. However, Sampson's son was uncontrollable from the start. Very impulsive boy. They tried everything they could to help him, but he ran away at the age of 16. No one has heard from him since then."

"So you think Seth took hold of him?" Kate asked.

"Yes," Millie nodded. "He's more Seth now than himself, if not completely Seth. Sampson also had a daughter, but she seemed much more serene. They claimed she had no birthmark and they never had a bit of trouble with the girl. She's a student at MIT."

Jonas froze, his fork halfway to his mouth. "Would her name be Liv?"

Millie nodded. "I had a feeling she was involved with Rob's death after I heard the girl he was with had gone missing, so I called the investigator. He confirmed that she was a student there since last semester."

"These beings, gods, whatever you want to call them; where are they from?"

"It's hard to say," Millie took a bite of ham and chewed thoughtfully. "They were known by many different names in many different lands, but their origins remain a mystery. Henry thought the secret probably lay in Atlantis."

"Henry believed in Atlantis?" Jonas asked. "It's no more than a fable."

"Your uncle didn't seem to think so. However, he also didn't think the issue that important. Once he knew Sampson's son was carrying Seth, he focused his attention on the myths surrounding Horus and Seth."

"What's Sampson's son's name?" Jonas asked.

"Horace."

"You're kidding?"

"No, dear. I guess they thought choosing something similar to Horus might help counteract his fate. Silly if you ask me. The poor child had enough going against him without a name like Horace."

"What about the student at the dig site?" Kate asked as she reached for a roll. "Whatever happened to him?"

"I don't know. I spent a lot of time looking for Raymond. About six years after we returned from Egypt, he was institutionalized and then released six months later. I haven't found a trace of him since then. If he sired any children, no one listed him as the birth father. I've had my private investigator keep checking, but there has never been a whisper of his whereabouts."

"How old would he be now?" Kate asked.

"Oh, mid fifties I should think."

"We need to talk to Professor Sampson," Jonas said.

"That might be difficult," Millie said, sipping her wine. "He died two weeks ago. As did his wife. Double suicide it seems."

"Right," Jonas said. "So you're the only confirmed living member of the group that went into that temple?"

"It would seem so."

CHAPTER 16

After dinner, Millie had retired to her room. The rest of their questions would have to wait until morning. While Burke napped on the rug in Jonas's room, Jonas took a shower and then went down the hall to Kate's room and knocked on the door.

"I was expecting you'd show up," she said. "Come in."

"You never told me what happened in the shower last night," Jonas said.

"I was hoping you'd forget." Kate closed the door behind him.

"Not a chance."

Kate sat on the bed and motioned for Jonas to join her. "It's complicated."

"Everything is complicated lately."

She nodded, taking a deep breath. "I was just standing there under the water. I was trying to think. And then suddenly I felt this presence in the room with me. It was strong. But even though I couldn't see him, I knew he was there. It was like staring at the light of an onrushing train, knowing you can't possibly get out of the way in time."

"He? The killer?"

"Yes. Seth. I knew it was him. He could see my thoughts, my feelings, but I could also see his. He was fascinated at first. As if he hadn't expected to find me, and then once he realized I could see into him, he vanished."

"Maybe there's some sort of support group for dysfunctional telepaths we could join," Jonas said.

"We wouldn't even have to talk. We could all just sit around and send each other creepy thoughts and images with our minds."

"Did you see anything? Feel anything? Something that might help us?" Jonas asked.

"I'm not sure. It's hard to explain. It didn't feel evil to me. It felt very volatile and full of chaotic energy, but I also felt this sense of being lost. Incomplete."

"Because he hasn't gained his full strength?"

"Maybe." Kate said.

Suddenly, realization struck Jonas. "You're a carrier too, aren't you?" he asked.

"Yes. I didn't know what it was until I met you and we started learning more, and then I didn't know who until yesterday morning. And I didn't know how until your aunt mentioned the archaeology student. He must have been my father."

"And which of our whacky gods do you get to have lurking inside you?"

"The cow," she mumbled.

"Hathor?" Jonas grinned. He looked her over. "You don't look like any cow I've ever seen."

"It's my serene personality. Comes from my inner cow."

"Good thing Greta made ham for dinner. Just think of the ramifications of eating a steak."

"It's never wise to offend your inner cow."

"Mine isn't so difficult. A hawk with anger issues."

"I was thinking about that," Kate said. "Out of all of us, you seem to have the least physical and emotional manifestations of your little guest. Other than the messages on the laptop and an urge to go places, you show no other signs."

"It's my unhealthy and yet useful ability to repress things," Jonas smiled. "Learned as a small child. I can pretty much repress any sort of ugly emotion I want to."

"That's quite a talent," Kate said. "And probably the reason you've held out so long."

"What about you? You don't strike me as odd."

"Hathor wasn't very odd. She seems to be a goddess of the arts. The only real part she played in the battle of Horus and Seth was when her father, Re, was in a bad mood and she stripped naked and danced around him until he was happy again. Though she did have a dark side."

"Oh?"

"Yeah," Kate said. "According to a tale known as 'The Destruction of Mankind' Sakhmet was a merciless aspect of Hathor's usual benign self, represented as a panther. Re sent Sakhmet to slay mortals who were plotting against him. Sakhmet became so enthralled with her task that she nearly slew all of humanity. Re prevented this by tricking her into drinking vast quantities of alcohol which he had colored to look like blood. The intoxicated goddess forgot what it was she was doing and went back to being Hathor, her sweet cow-headed self."

"So if you throw a fit, I just have to get you a few beers?" Jonas asked.

"I guess so," she smiled.

"And what do I have to do to get to the dancing naked part?"

"Maybe if you looked a bit gloomier," Kate said.

"Not sure I can do gloomy. Would brooding suffice?"

"Close enough."

※ ※ ※

Millie sat in her bedroom, sipping her tea and staring into the fireplace. She wondered if she should have told Jonas the rest. It was difficult keeping something important from him, but she didn't know who else might have access to his thoughts.

She would do whatever she could to help and protect him, but in the end only he would be able to make the choices that won or lost the battle for all of them. With the help of Kate and Burke, however, he might just make it through.

She must be the one to guide him, however. She couldn't leave that up to Burke and Kate. Jonas still viewed the situation with the human perspective and that wouldn't do. He had to see that there was only one solution to this problem and only one way in which to accomplish it.

She had spent many years waiting for this day. Now that it was finally here she felt ill prepared to deal with it. Jonas wasn't what they had expected. She had told them that the boy might be difficult to deal with at first, but she had been assured that it would be taken care of. It obviously hadn't been taken care of yet. She would have to do it herself.

None of them knew how this would play out, but Millie had the feeling that the ending to this long tale was going to be one that was highly unexpected.

🍁   🍁   🍁

Jonas grabbed Kate by the waist, pulling her to him. He could no longer stand the torture of not touching her bare flesh. His lips caught hers in a devouring kiss as his hands roamed over the silken skin of her back.

Her lips left his and she trailed a line of kisses down his neck. "You're still dressed," she murmured against his skin.

"Am I?"

"Mhmm."

"We should do something about that."

Kate slid the sweater over his head along with the T-shirt underneath. She ran her hands over the muscled contours of his chest and over the flat plain of his belly to the button of his jeans. She placed a kiss on the center of his chest as she unfastened them and slid them down his long legs.

His hands clenched into fists at his sides as anticipation welled within him. Just as he moved his hands to her head, she took him into her mouth, and searing heat shot through his loins.

His fingers tangled in her hair as she moved her lips slowly across his length. He moaned in male pleasure. Kate sucked him deep within her mouth, feeling his hardened shaft touch the back of her throat. As she pulled back, she let her tongue wrap around the end, tasting the salty essence of him.

He was beautiful, Kate thought. Never had she thought a man beautiful before she had seen Jonas lying naked upon his bed sheathed in moonlight at the hotel. Every inch of him was sleekly muscled and built for speed, strength, and endurance. He was like a panther, graceful yet deadly.

Jonas closed his eyes, reaching out to grab the windowsill for support. A sparkling electrical current seemed to race along each nerve ending. He wasn't going to last much longer.

Every touch, every sensation seemed magnified a hundredfold. A plethora of erotic images from a different time and place flashed through his mind. He was powerless to stop the shockwave that overtook him, unable to utter a single sound while his body shuddered and convulsed. Kate's lips didn't leave him until the last tremor passed.

His knees grew weak, and Kate wrapped an arm about his waist as he slid to his knees before her. She pulled him close and he laid his head on her shoulder, too drained to lift his arms. The sweet smell of her calmed him, and his breathing slowly evened out. He had no idea what had just happened to him, but it was far more than it should have been.

He drew back and cupped her cheek as he looked at her. Her eyes seemed to sparkle with a golden light that glittered like stars on a clear night. He brushed his lips against hers, savoring the taste of her as he threaded his fingers through her hair.

"I think it's bed time," he said.

"Tired already?"

"Hardly."

❦   ❦   ❦

Reamun sat outside the mansion, hidden by the shadows of dense foliage surrounding the estate. Things were happening. He felt energies converging. He could feel the ball of twine being undone.

His cell phone vibrated and he answered it. "Yes?"

"Where is he?" Liv asked.

"I have not felt him all day," Reamun said. "But do not worry yourself. If he were up to something, I would know."

"You're so sure," she scoffed. "You underestimate him. Just as you underestimate Jonas."

"I know their limits."

"Do you?" she asked.

Reamun paused. She was getting at something and it disturbed him that she was not being forthcoming.

"Do you know where I am?" he asked. "I'm in Georgia. Right outside a beautiful mansion."

"You aren't going to interfere are you?" Liv's voice was suddenly full of panic.

"Ah, you still care about her."

"Was there any doubt? Just stay out of it, Reamun. You know your continued interference will only cause upheaval and more conflict. You cannot play them as pawns any longer. Let them choose their own course as it should have been from the beginning."

"We did what had to be done to save this realm from chaos."

"We did it to serve our own purposes. As we still do. Stay away, Reamun. They will bring about the final solution on their own."

"We shall see."

🍁   🍁   🍁

I walk in darkness. I need no light to see where I am going. Clouds obscure the waning moon, shielding it from my sight. I can feel the Other now without any effort. I am unsure if this means that my powers are near their pinnacle or if the Other's powers have grown significantly.

The Other is strange to me. Unlike everyone else, he has kept his human counterpart fully intact. He is now aware, at least in part, of his destined role and yet still he remains steadfast. I do not discount this as foolish as some may. If he is able to retain control of his human mind while calling upon the hidden powers within, then he will be an altogether different foe to contend with.

I move soundlessly through the night as I seek out my victim. Unlike the others, this victim is of my choosing alone. No source of fate or grand design leads me on this task. I will no longer play the game by their rules.

My newly found ability to conceal myself is proving to be useful. I am not certain that it will hold out against the full power of the Other, but meeting such power may never come to pass.

All those who are seeking me out will be met with silence and darkness. They do not comprehend me or my powers. Though my sister knows and understands me better than most, even she has no true idea of what dwells within me. They are all blind. They will all pay the price for their ignorance.

Only the Other has ever truly known me. Had he not been so easily swayed by the lies and deceit of those who claimed to care for him, we would not have come to this terrible end. It is something that cannot be changed. Though it grieves me, I have no great fear of the outcome. Only the Other can stop me now. We are bound by our fates, by our hate, by our love.

I slip past all the carefully laid security with ease. I walk down the darkened corridors making no sound as I pass emptied rooms. As I draw nearer to my destination, I feel a surge of intense anticipation. If the Other were to seek me out now and realize the peril, he will have the chance to thwart my plans.

This does not worry me. Instead, I almost yearn for him to confront me. To feel his glorious rage. The thrill of danger heightens my anticipation.

CHAPTER 17

❀

Jonas woke in the night to the sound of thunder, a scream caught in his throat. He let out his breath slowly, trying to calm himself.

Kate stirred beside him. "What is it? Bad dream?"

"Yes," he said, and then "No." He climbed out of bed, grabbing his pants from the floor and sliding them on as he hopped across the room.

"Jonas?" Kate sat up, still half asleep.

"He's here," Jonas said. "He's going after Millie. Hide."

"The hell I will," she said. She stood and grabbed her robe.

"No, Kate. Stay here. He won't hurt me. Not yet. But he'll use you against me if he can. Hide. I'll send Burke. The two of you go get Greta."

She knew he was right. She hated that she couldn't help him, but she wouldn't knowingly hinder him either. "Okay. Take the gun," she said. She dug the Glock out of her bag and handed it to him. "Be careful."

Jonas nodded and then quietly crept from the room. He first went to check on Burke and found the dog pawing at the door. Jonas knelt so that he was at Burke's level as he spoke through the door.

"Listen to me, pal. I need you to hide. Let me handle this. Can you do that?"

Chuff.

"No doggy tricks. You go straight to Kate and hide with her. I need you both safe."

Chuff.

Jonas opened the door and Burke gazed up at him for a moment. Jonas nodded, and Burke ran off in the direction of Kate's room. Jonas continued down the hallway and began ascending the steps to the third floor where his aunt's room was.

As he reached the third floor landing, he heard a noise that seemed to come from Millie's room. He approached the door cautiously and eased it open with his left hand while holding the gun awkwardly in his right.

The light from the bathroom illuminated the empty bed, but most of the room was still cast in shadow. He heard a noise in the bathroom and moved to the half-open door and looked inside.

He saw no movement near the bathtub, but the other half of the bathroom was out of his line of sight. He took a breath and then stepped inside, swinging the gun to what had been his blind spot, but finding nothing there. Turning back toward the tub, he aimed the gun at the door.

No attacker stood in the doorway waiting for him, but when his eyes fell upon the bathtub again, he saw that Millie lay submerged beneath the water, eyes open wide in death. He suppressed the scream of rage that threatened to tear from his throat and went back out into the bedroom. He made himself focus. He couldn't save Millie now, but he could save Burke and Kate.

He switched on the bedroom light. There was no sign of the attacker. He walked back out into the hallway and headed for the stairs. Just as he reached the landing, he was tackled from behind, the weight of his attacker sending him to the ground and pinning the gun beneath his body.

"You have been searching for me a long time," a deep voice, low and smooth as honey whispered from above him.

"You aren't going to get away forever," Jonas said.

"It is not yet time for us," the voice whispered in his ear. "But soon enough."

"She was a defenseless old lady," Jonas hissed as his mind raced, trying to figure out a way to get the upper hand.

A mirthless laugh issued from the other man. It was a dry grating sound. "She has been the bane of my existence for thousands of years. She was anything but defenseless."

"You're mad. She was an old woman. She never hurt anyone."

"She truly didn't tell you then?" the voice whispered. Jonas could feel the heat of his breath against his neck. "It doesn't surprise me. Though you were her beloved son, she was never above deceiving you to gain her own ends. They always worshipped Isis as such a divine goddess of good. In truth, she was as wicked and self-serving as the rest of them."

"She would have told me," Jonas said, struggling to get free.

"Would she? Do not be blind to her wiles as you always were. See her in death as you refused to see her in life. I have done you a favor, though you know it not. The coroner will find she has died of a heart attack and subsequent drowning. You will not be suspected."

"You've done me no favors."

"We shall see how you feel when next we meet. Farewell, great falcon."

Suddenly, the weight was gone from his back and Jonas rolled, bringing up the gun but the attacker was gone. Jonas ran to Millie's room and found the window open, the curtains billowing in the night breeze.

He ran to the window, looking out into the night, but saw only darkness. He was gone. Jonas's hands clenched at his sides. He had failed yet again.

CHAPTER 18

When the police left and Millie's body had been taken away, and the calls had been made to the funeral home that Millie had picked out for herself years ago, Jonas sat in silence with Burke on the patio and stared out into the gardens. Kate was inside consoling Greta. He hadn't told the police about the attacker. He was certain there would be no evidence for them to find and that such a tale would only cause them to be suspicious of Jonas, who was the only heir to Millie's half of the massive Uhrig fortune.

He had waited until morning to call them, making it plausible that they had missed her at breakfast and he went to go wake her. It had been a painful lie, but he had pulled it off with surprising ease. They hadn't asked many questions. She was over seventy after all, and a call to her physician confirmed Greta's assertion that she had a weak heart.

Jonas sat thinking of what the killer had said. If it were true, and Millie had been carrying Isis, why wouldn't she tell him? All the others who had been in that tomb had children who were carriers. Except for Millie and Henry. He still had difficulty believing any of it, but it all fit so perfectly that there could be no other explanation.

He wished he had notes and photographs from the site to look through, but the Egyptian government had taken them all. Unless Henry had written down his experience somewhere.

He had seen his Uncle's library many times and knew the man had taken precise notes on every site he had ever worked. He recorded every last detail regardless of the fact that it was seemingly inconsequential. He would have written something down, even if he didn't have any of the original notes. Even if he could never publish his findings.

"Come on, Burke. Let's go have a look at Henry's library."

🍁 🍁 🍁

Kate found Jonas an hour later surrounded by journals and stacks of paper. Burke was sitting next to him, looking slightly bewildered. "Greta is taking a nap. Want some lunch?"

Jonas shook his head and continued sifting through the piles, scanning each piece before setting it aside.

"What are you doing?"

"Has to be here somewhere," Jonas muttered.

"What has to be here?"

"Notes."

"Notes?"

"Henry's notes on the temple," Jonas said.

"But Millie said they were taken."

"Henry would have written new ones as soon as he returned. He was meticulous that way."

"Wouldn't Millie have told us that?"

"Maybe. Maybe not," Jonas said.

"That would be important, don't you think? She wouldn't just leave that out," Kate said.

"No. Unless she didn't want us to know everything."

"That doesn't make sense."

"I know he would have had notes, Kate. Maybe she was just too tired and forgot. Maybe she had a reason for not telling us last night. I don't know. I just know they have to be here somewhere."

"Alright," Kate relented. "I'll help you look, but you need to eat something. I'll make sandwiches so we can eat while we look, okay?"

"Fine," Jonas turned his attention once again to the stacks surrounding him. Kate went into the kitchen and made sandwiches, slicing some apples as well and making a plate of just meat for Burke. When she went back into the library, Jonas was pulling more volumes off the shelves.

After being certain that he ate, Kate dove into the piles with him and began the search for Henry's account of what had happened in that sanctuary in Egypt so long ago.

They searched for two more hours before Kate finally stood and stretched. "I don't think they're here, Jonas."

"They have to be."

"We've looked through nearly everything here."

Jonas looked up at her. She was right, but he knew the notes existed. "I have to find them."

"What if he didn't want them to be found? Would he keep them in his library?"

"Maybe not," Jonas thought for a moment. "He kept important papers like his will and things in the safe in his room."

"Do you know the combination?"

"Yeah. The date of his and Millie's wedding anniversary."

"Not very original," Kate said.

"Millie said it gave him an added incentive to remember the date," Jonas smiled.

"Did he ever forget?"

"Not a single year."

Kate and Burke followed Jonas upstairs. When Jonas opened the safe, he found a copy of Millie's will, birth certificates, death certificates for Henry and both of Jonas's parents, four thousand dollars in cash, but no papers or old journals that might be connected to the temple.

"Where else would he hide it?" Kate asked.

"This house is so huge. It could be anywhere."

"What if he didn't want Millie to know about it? It would explain why she didn't tell us. If he had some reason to keep it from her, but leave it for you, where would it be?"

Jonas thought for a moment. He had been very young when Henry had died, but he had fond memories of what little time they had spent together. Inspiration suddenly struck. "The chess board."

"Chess board?"

"Yes. It's one of the things we always did when I was here. Henry would spend hours teaching me to play chess. He let me beat him once and then never again. I had to earn it."

"Did you?"

"Twice, but we must have played hundreds of games over the years. It was a really beautiful marble board with jade figurines for pieces. He used to keep it on a shelf next to his writing desk."

They went back downstairs to the small room off the library where the writing desk sat surrounded by shelves full of artifacts and fossils. On the center of the bottom shelf was the chess board, just as Jonas remembered it.

He lifted each figure off the board and then inspected the board itself. On the underside was a small compartment where the figures could be stored. When he opened it, he found a key taped inside. He lifted it out, feeling as if he had found some precious treasure.

"It's a safe deposit box key," Jonas said.

"Nothing in there indicating where the safe deposit box was at?"

"No," Jonas said. "And it isn't mentioned in the will either."

"What about an attorney? Someone with an estate this large would have one to handle mundane affairs, wouldn't they?" Kate asked.

"Yeah. I should meet with him anyway. I'll give him a call."

❦   ❦   ❦

Thomas Carlisle sat behind his large oak desk looking suitably distressed after hearing of Millie's death. Apparently it was the talk of the town and Carlisle was always sure that he was aware of what went on in the small town of Fallwood. A potential client was behind every land purchase and mishap.

"I'm very sorry, Jonas. She was a dear woman."

Jonas, aware that all good lawyers were good actors as well, didn't actually believe Carlisle was sorry about anything other than losing a paying client, but he held his tongue. Jonas merely nodded, not wanting to think about it. If he stopped to think about everyone he had lost in the past week, he would fall apart.

"Her will leaves everything to you, of course. It shouldn't take too long to get all the paperwork done. She made sure that the preparations were all made ahead of time."

"There was a key to a safe deposit box at the house. The will makes no mention of it. Do you know what bank that was at?"

"A safe deposit box?" Carlisle looked perplexed as he shuffled through the file. "No. No mention of it. Millie had accounts with two Atlanta banks, but I would think that she would want to use one of the local banks for a safe deposit box, don't you?"

"Probably," Jonas said.

"Let's see," Carlisle shuffled through some more papers. "There are only two banks in Fallwood. Let me call them and see what I can find out."

Jonas waited patiently while Carlisle spoke in hushed tones into the telephone. When he hung up, he looked at Jonas with a smile of satisfaction.

"The safe deposit box is indeed right here in town. It's at Fallwood Bank and Trust. Apparently it was Henry who opened it, not Millie. They'll be expecting you so you shouldn't have any trouble at all."

"Thank you," Jonas said as he stood.

"Is there anything else I can do for you, Mr. Uhrig?"

"Yes, actually. You can draw up my own will. Everything is to be sold in the event of my death and the entire sum is to be set up in a trust fund to provide scholarships to the local townsfolk."

Carlisle's eyes widened. "All of it?"

"I have no family left, Mr. Carlisle. In the event that changes at some point in the future, my will may also change."

"Of course," he said. "I'll draw it up and have it sent for you to sign."

"Thank you."

Jonas left, trying not to run out to the car though his sense of urgency was building. He got into the BMW M5 which had been his aunt's, though she never used it. He didn't even think she had a driver's license. Gregor had driven her everywhere she needed to go.

Greta had used the car occasionally when her own wasn't running to do errands and shop for groceries. Jonas planned to give her the title to the vehicle as soon as he was done with it. He never liked expensive cars. Though he had the money to spend, it seemed like such a silly waste to spend it on something like a vehicle. Comfort and quality could be found just as easily in a twenty-five thousand dollar car as it could in one that was seventy thousand.

He drove down Main Street, the bank was only two blocks from the attorney's office. A variety of shops and stores lined the entire street. All of them in the same quaint southern small town style. There wasn't a single flashing neon light on the entire stretch. No electronic signs with lights heralding bargains. The signs were simply painted and during evening hours lit by soft light.

Fallwood had strict guidelines when it came to development. The townsfolk liked their community quiet and clean and did whatever they could to keep the encroaching metropolis at bay.

When he walked into the bank, the bank manager was there to greet him. Mrs. Fulkom was a small round woman in her mid fifties with grey hair pulled up neatly in a bun that sat atop her head. She wore a modest wool suit and had a grandmotherly look of concern on her face. She held a handkerchief in her hands and was wringing it back and forth. She had been one of Millie's few close friends, and Jonas had no doubt about her sincerity.

"Oh, you poor boy," she said. "We're all really very sorry to hear about Millie. She was such a good woman. I don't know what to say."

"It's alright, Mrs. Fulkom. I haven't really had time to absorb it yet."

"Oh, of course you haven't. These things take time. Will you be staying at the estate until the funeral?"

"I'm not sure," Jonas said honestly. "I hadn't thought that far ahead."

"Silly me," she said as she patted his shoulder. "The last thing you need is an old woman asking you questions. Mr. Carlisle said you wanted to see the safe deposit box. I had nearly forgotten the thing. Henry opened it so long ago. Just before he died, in fact."

"I'd like to see it. I thought maybe it would have some of my uncle's things in there."

"Yes, of course."

She lead him down a hallway and then down a flight of stairs. Their footsteps echoed hollowly in the stairwell. The light was dim and Jonas had the feeling they were descending into a tomb. Shadows danced along the walls as they moved.

Once they found the box, and Jonas produced the key, she left him to open the box with the admonishment that he let her know if he needed anything.

Jonas stood in front of the small counter, staring down at the box. When he opened it, he found a large manila envelope, slightly worn with age. He lifted it gently from the box and opened it. Inside was a leather-bound journal. There were two words etched into the front with gold foil. *For Jonas.* He ran his fingers along the letters, at once inexplicably gripped by a deep sadness. He opened the journal to the first page. His uncle's flowing script was there, and printed in large bold strokes were the words 'The Account of the Lost Sanctuary of the Gods Near Idfu, Egypt. 1966'.

Resisting the urge to read further, he closed the journal and slipped it back into the envelope and hurried up the steps. Circumventing Mrs. Fulkom who was in conversation with a bank patron, he slipped out the door and got into the BMW, his heart racing.

He did his best to stick to the speed limit as he made his way back to the estate where Kate and Burke were waiting. Soon they would know everything that Millie and Henry knew about the expedition that had left them all under the shadow of a strange curse.

CHAPTER 19

Reamun stared out at the rolling landscape beyond the window of his hotel room. She was dead. He could hardly believe it. He had never thought that Seth would have the audacity, the utmost disrespect for all that was sacred to commit such an act. He had killed one of their own.

It hadn't been the first time he had done so, but this time his act was irreversible. Upon killing Osiris in the past days of their glory, he had been resurrected as the god of the Underworld. It had not meant the end for Osiris. In this deed, there was no going back. Her fate was locked with that of the human body she possessed, as the fates of all of them were until the battle was ended. She was lost to this realm forever.

"You should have seen this," Liv said, her voice breaking as she sobbed. She sat on the floor nearby. She had arrived early this morning, her face a mask of anger and misery.

"He loved her. I had no idea. I did not think…"

"He hated her! She was the cause of much of his pain. Yes he once loved her, but those are days long past. She deceived him far too many times, she sought only to break his spirit and crush him. She turned Horus from him."

And that, Reamun thought, had been the deed that had most cut him. Seth could have borne many things, but the separation of

Horus and the battles that had come after had been something he would find unforgivable.

"He has killed your dearest friend and yet you defend him," Reamun said.

"He is like a wounded animal. Can you not see that? He strikes out in pain and fear. You and the others are responsible for making him what he is. You have driven him to it."

"And you?"

She hung her head. "I am also to blame, though I wish it were otherwise."

"He must be stopped. None of us is now safe."

"Only one can stop him," she said. "And if he fails, we will all face the judgment of Seth."

"Then we must see that he does not fail."

"No," Liv said. "No more interference. It will only add to the chaos."

"You dare to gainsay me?" Reamun asked.

"You do not have the power you once had, and you will not again until this is finished. Unlike you, I did not turn a blind eye to all the pain the conflict caused in them. Their wounds run deep, and it is the fire from those wounds that fuels them now. If you continue to meddle, the outcome could very well be worse for us all."

🍁 🍁 🍁

When Jonas returned to the house, Kate and Burke were anxiously waiting just inside the front door.

"Did you get it?" she asked.

"Got it. Looks like Henry had a great deal to say on the subject. The journal he left is at least fifty pages."

"Let's hope it has some answers," Kate said.

They went into the drawing room and sat huddled on the couch as Jonas opened the journal. He flipped past the title page and found that between it and the first page was a letter to him from Henry. It had been folded and tucked inside.

April 17, 1975

Dearest Jonas,

If you're reading this, I'm dead and likely so is my beloved Millie. You also likely know what is happening to some extent, but Millie wouldn't have told you the whole story. I have seen signs lately that she is becoming one of them. Perhaps if we'd had a child, the burden would have shifted elsewhere, but having no other place to manifest, the goddess has taken her place within Millie and she isn't strong enough to resist giving into Isis for very long.

I had foolishly thought that we would avoid it by not having any children, but it seems I was wrong. I was wrong about a lot of things in my life, but this one thing I will try to do right, even if I'm not there to help you in body.

You hold within you one of the most powerful gods of the ancient world. Whether these beings are truly gods or some life form beyond our comprehension, I'm not sure. Nor do I really think it matters in the end.

In the pages of my journal you will find the writings we saw in the sanctuary and my own observations. These will give you a basis for what is supposed to happen. However, in the research I have done, I have found that not all is what it seems.

Seth is held up as evil, and I have no doubt that he has committed some very regrettable acts. Horus is held up as being the avenger, the light, the true hero. I have no doubt that you have shown these qualities as well.

But you must not hold to these as binding truths. The history of these two gods is far more complex than it seems on the surface and you must find a solution that will be fitting for both of you.

Every single one of these deities has their own ulterior motives. I do not believe you can fully trust any of them, but from what I have learned the two most likely to be in your corner alone are Hathor and Thoth. Hathor was Horus's wife and Thoth his son as well as the son of Seth. They will want to protect him, to protect you. They will be drawn to you, and they will help you. Trust no one else. Not even what Millie has told you.

I wish I had a final solution to give you, but in the past nine years, I haven't come up with one that would put everything back to rights. I only know that you must try not to let Horus take hold of you. Learn from him, feel his thoughts, but the solution must come from you alone.

All my love and hopes,

Henry

Jonas read the letter twice, feeling slightly dizzy. Millie had been Isis. Jonas wondered what it was that made Henry warn him against trusting her. In all the accounts they had read, she was a gentle and loving goddess, though she had made mistakes.

"Well, at least I'm not one of the ones out to get you," Kate said. "But he's right. If Hathor were to take more control over me, you shouldn't trust even me."

Jonas looked at Burke. "And you?"

Chuff. Burke licked his face and grinned at him.

"You don't act like any god I've ever heard of."

Burke gave him puppy dog eyes and nudged the letter down flat upon the book. He then placed his nose on a single word. Thoth.

"Your're Thoth?"

The dog whimpered and then chuffed softly.

"You've got a little Thoth in you but you aren't really Thoth like I'm not really Horus?"

Chuff.

"Okay, then. Now that we have that settled, let's see what we can find in the journal."

🍁   🍁   🍁

Though the small group who had entered the sanctuary had been inside for only a short while, Henry had been able to get an overall idea from what he himself had witnessed and what the others had told him.

The most prominent figure in the sanctuary seemed to be the god Re, who was overlooking the others, presumably in protection of their souls. The others who were prominently featured were Horus and Hathor, Seth and Nephthys, Isis, and Thoth. Osiris had been depicted below these figures looking upward as if awaiting the outcome.

The story of Horus and Seth had been inscribed on one wall. Henry had only gotten part way through it when the lights had gone out, but he had seen enough to realize that current belief about the nature of the relationship between the two was almost entirely off base.

Though a sexual encounter between the two gods was widely known, it seemed that there was more to it than anyone had imagined. The two had both been born out of balance. For the way to be cleared for Horus to take his rightful place, Osiris had to die and be reborn as god of the Underworld, leaving room for Horus. Knowing this, Seth murdered his brother against the will of the other gods.

For this the other gods shunned him and made him an outcast. Though in time, Horus came to accept it. The bond between the two gods was strong. They were lovers, companions, and confidants.

Fearing the chaos that would come about from the binding of the two gods whose births had brought imbalance to the world, Isis and others conspired to turn them away from one another. The wars and battles that followed would make them enemies. Horus lost his eye to Seth and Seth his seed to Horus not from battle, but from the separation of the two gods from one another.

Modern texts contained a wealth of information about the Eye of Horus, but they contain little about the testicles of Seth, which seem to be just as important. This didn't surprise Jonas. He could imagine the discomfort in a room full of scholars expounding on the symbolism of disembodied testicles.

From Henry's notes, he found that the Eye represents the light, the testicles represent sexuality, and both combined represent fertility and bountifulness.

"Maybe I'm missing something," Kate said. "But it seems to me that separating them brought about more chaos than them being together."

"That's how it appears," Jonas said.

He continued reading. Bits of various texts on Egyptian mythology were scattered throughout the pages. As he read, traces of ancient memory flashed through his mind filling in the gaps. Jonas began to see a pattern emerge. One that was both fascinating and frightening.

"What are you thinking?" Kate asked.

"I'm thinking there is a way to solve this that doesn't end in any sort of battle."

"How?"

"I have to think about it some more. It isn't clear yet. I need to let it all sink in. I also have to find Seth."

"And how are you going to do that?"

"If Horace Sampson is completely taken over by Seth, then he will have wanted to keep tabs on me. So far he has been leading me around as he kills the people I care about. I have to turn the tables. I have to bring him to me."

※　　　※　　　※

I feel the sun on my face as I look toward the house in which the Other now sits remembering. The light is unlike the brilliance of the light that I once knew. It is hazy and unwelcoming. Though it warms the skin, it does not touch my heart. I prefer the darkness of this world. In the darkness I can see only that which I wish to see.

The Other is so close that I feel I can reach out and touch him. He is growing in power, though he is not one. He divides himself into two within his body and yet he still grows in strength.

He feels me here, though he isn't aware how close I am. He feels the longings of my heart and the chaos of my mind. He begins to know me once more. This frightens and thrills me as it frightens and thrills the Other.

I cannot now separate his thoughts to clearly read what he is thinking. He is shielding himself from the outside world as I have done. I know he is planning, plotting, remembering. He is my one true equal and a most admirable foe.

I wait for him to lead me to my next level. I am curious to see what he will do. Will he know me? He will attempt to thwart me. He will believe he can beat me at my own game. He is wrong.

I turn from the house, walking back into the sheltering darkness of the trees to await the twilight.

※ ※ ※

"Why Raiden? Why not use me?" Kate asked.

"Because he hasn't even tried for you or Burke yet. He's had opportunity. I think he's saving you for last."

"How flattering," Kate said. "The best for last."

"He won't get that far," Jonas said.

"So Raiden is on the way?"

"Yeah. He's coming from South Carolina, so it shouldn't be too long," Jonas said.

"And he agreed to this crazy scheme?"

"Raiden would go for just about anything that gave him an adrenaline rush."

"The whole risk of death thing doesn't scare him?" Kate asked.

"Doubtful. Or maybe it's the fear that he gets off on. I don't know. He's strange that way. Bungee jumping, skydiving, you name it," Jonas said.

"Are you sure this plan of yours is going to work?"

"I'll make it work. We should get some rest before he arrives. Neither of us slept much last night and I doubt we'll be sleeping much tonight either."

"Good idea. I'll go tell Greta to wake us if he gets here before we wake up."

Jonas went up to his room with Burke following quietly while Kate went to find Greta. He was more tired than he could ever remember being in his entire life. He felt worn to the point of breaking. He managed to kick his shoes off before falling onto the bed. By the time Kate came in the room only minutes later, he was fast asleep. She crawled in next to him and wrapped her arms around him. She was afraid she would never get the chance to do so again. She wondered how they were ever going to find a way out of the madness they had stepped into.

CHAPTER 20

Kate woke to find Jonas staring out the window. She climbed out of bed and went to his side.

"Nervous?"

"A little," Jonas said. He pulled her close and kissed the top of her head. "But everything will work out. As long as Raiden agrees to it."

"That must be him," Kate said, indicating the car coming down the driveway.

Jonas went downstairs and out onto the porch. He watched as Raiden hopped out of the car, slinging a small backpack over his shoulder. He looked no more concerned than if he were attending a hockey game.

"Nice place," Raiden said. "You told me your aunt lived in a big house, but you never said it was this big. You could probably house the entire town in there."

"Only twenty bedrooms," Jonas said.

"Only?"

"Are you going to stand there gawking or are you coming in?"

"Oh, I'm coming in. And you're going to tell me what the hell is going on."

While Kate helped Greta make dinner, Jonas filled Raiden in on the details. It wasn't so much that Greta needed the help as Kate needed to keep herself occupied. Kate knew Greta would probably prefer to do it alone, but she had graciously accepted Kate's offer of help in preparing the meal.

Kate's thoughts shifted to Jonas and Raiden. Though their personalities seemed to be entirely different, their friendship was a close one. She envied them. She had never had a close friend to share all her secrets with.

Jonas had only given her the barest outline of his plan. She wasn't sure if he didn't want her to know the details or if he wasn't sure of them himself.

Chuff.

Kate looked down to see Burke staring longingly at the pot roast she was cutting. "You're going to give me the puppy dog eyes if I don't give you some, aren't you?"

Burke flashed a pathetic doggy look, complete with soulful eyes before grinning at her.

Kate laughed. "You don't play fair," she said. She put some roast on a napkin and set it on the floor.

Burke licked her hand in gratitude before eating.

"He's a good dog, that one. The puppy dog eyes don't work on me though. That's why he goes to you," Greta said.

"I was always a pushover."

Kate washed her hands, her mind still on the conversation Raiden and Jonas were having in the study. She wanted to know what they were up to, but she also didn't want to pry. If Jonas didn't want her to know, then he had his reasons.

"This friend of Jonas's," Greta said. "He is going to help him?"

"Hopefully. How much of this do you know?"

"Just what I have heard over the years. Voices tend to carry in such a large house."

※　　　※　　　※

Raiden looked at Jonas over the rim of the glass of whiskey he was currently imbibing. His emerald eyes held no surprise, merely a hint of curiosity. "If he isn't jealous of Kate, what makes you think he'll be jealous of me?"

"It's different," Jonas said.

"I'll say. For you, at least." Raiden downed the rest of the glass and stood to pour himself another.

"For me? But not you? You do this kind of thing a lot? Trying to dupe ancient gods with illusions of lust must be taxing. It's a wonder you have energy for all those women," Jonas said.

"Not the ancient gods thing, and they aren't all women," Raiden said.

Jonas stared at him a moment, unable to speak.

"You're surprised?"

"No," Jonas said and it was the truth. "I just hadn't ever considered it."

"You wouldn't."

"Are you saying I'm a prude?"

"Yes."

"You're right," Jonas smiled. "I am. You never mentioned anything. How was I to know?"

"You weren't. I thought you might get all atwitter and weird on me," Raiden grinned. He sat back down in the wingchair across from Jonas.

"Atwitter?" Jonas asked with mock horror. "When have I ever been atwitter?"

Raiden shrugged. "You seem like the twittering sort."

"I don't twitter."

"Twitch maybe?"

Jonas laughed. "Very rarely."

"I'd suggest spasm, but that brings all sorts of other things to mind," Raiden winked.

"Indeed."

"Wouldn't want you twitching. Kate would surely kick me out."

"I don't know. She seems to enjoy making me twitch," Jonas sighed.

"Does she, now?"

"But we have more important things to discuss."

"More important than the twitching?"

"People could be killed," Jonas said.

"Yes," Raiden nodded. "People like me."

"You don't have to do this."

"I want to. It's the opportunity of a lifetime."

"It's insane," Jonas said.

"Just my thing," Raiden raised his glass in a salute before taking another drink.

"You don't seem to have any trouble believing all this," Jonas said.

"I figure that if you're a wacko and killing everyone yourself, I could probably kick your ass. If you're right about all this, then it's pretty damn weird. I'm all for weird."

"I just have to figure out where to stash Greta, Kate and Burke," Jonas said.

"Why stash 'em anywhere? You make it look like they left and then they can hide somewhere in the house. That way they're close at hand if you need them or they need you."

"Why didn't I think of that?" Jonas asked.

"Because you're trying too hard. You need to relax. He'll know something is up if you don't."

"Easier said than done."

"You'll give yourself an ulcer before this is over."

"Ulcers are the least of my worries."

"Relax, Jonas. This will either work like a charm or he won't show up at all."

There was a knock on the door. "Dinner," Kate said.

❦ ❦ ❦

"Why can't I figure out who she is?" Reamun asked.

"Maybe she's just who she appears to be," Liv said.

"No. She's one of us. I can feel it. I just don't know which one of us she is."

He paced to the window, looking out at the sky as if it held the answers. It had seemed unimportant before, but now he had to know who she was and what role she would play. Many would aid them, but there were a few who might be guided by motivations of their own to see Seth win.

"Why are you so worried? No one else is important in the grand scheme of things."

"No one else was important to the battles maybe, but if she's a target of Seth's, I wish to know whom he is targeting."

"Could be anyone. Tefnut, Hathor, Naunet…"

"*Hathor*," Reamun said. "Only my wayward daughter could hide from me so well."

"The woman would have to be a child of one of the people in the group who entered the sanctuary."

"So she is," Reamun said.

"Whose?"

"Mine. I had a girlfriend before I was committed all those years ago. When they finally released me, there was no sign of her. She'd helped my parents get the order of commitment against me. For so long she refused to help them, but then something changed her mind. If she found out she was pregnant, she would have feared for the child."

"Were you crazy?" Liv asked.

"Perhaps I was. I didn't know what was happening to me. I had heard that the Uhrig woman and Professor Sampson had children with strange birthmarks, but none of us had shown any signs."

"Why did she stay with you at all?"

"She and I had been together since high school. She wanted to believe it would pass. It was good that they sent me away, though. In my drug-induced haze I could no longer fight off the inevitable."

"That was when you merged with Re?"

"I became Re. There is little of Raymond left. Unlike you, I did not cling to my humanity."

"I find it gives me perspective," Liv said. "So now that you know she is not only the daughter of Re, but the human daughter of Raymond, what will you do?"

"If Seth has figured this out, he will want to kill her. I must protect her."

"Jonas is protecting her," Liv said.

"It isn't enough."

"If he fails to protect her from Seth, then he cannot hope to protect himself and it will make no difference. He cares for her. He would give his life for her. Can you say the same?"

Reamun glowered, turning away. "He is still torn. His focus will be elsewhere. I must go to her."

"She won't welcome you," Liv said. "If you must protect her, do it from afar. Do not interfere."

"As long as she is in no danger, I will not interfere. Come. We have things to do."

CHAPTER 21

Raiden handed his keys to Kate. "Do your worst. It's a rental."

"Thanks. Always wanted to see how fast a Saturn could go."

"Once you're sure you aren't being followed, just drive the car to the north end of the property and make your way back. You have a flashlight?" Jonas asked.

Kate patted her satchel. "Yep. And doggy snacks, and bottled water, and my Glock, and my cell phone, and a fruit roll-up."

"Fruit roll-up?" Raiden asked.

"I figure gods have to be tempted by something. Maybe that something is pressed fruit sheets," Kate grinned.

"Good thinking," Raiden nodded. "Though I would have thought it was Jolly Ranchers."

"That hadn't occurred to me. I'll have to hope the Fruit roll-ups work in a bind."

"Where's Burke?" Jonas asked.

"In the kitchen. He's been there all night. Hovering over the pot roast," Greta said.

"Actually, he seems worried about something. Probably your insane scheme," Kate said.

"He doesn't know my insane scheme," Jonas said.

"Maybe *that* is why he's mopey."

"I'll go get him," Jonas grumbled as he headed for the kitchen. "You just continue making light of things while I develop my ulcer a little more."

"Will do," Raiden said.

"He's really worried, isn't he?" Kate asked after Jonas left the room.

"Yep, but it's a good plan. He's a worrier," Raiden said.

"You think his plan will work?"

"Yes, I do."

"But you aren't going to tell me what it is, are you?" Kate asked.

"Not a chance. Just come in the east entrance from the gardens when you hike your way back and stay in the solarium. Greta will drive the car back in a few hours. We'll take care of the rest."

"Do you have a gun?"

"Of course," Raiden said, patting his jacket.

"Does Jonas know that?"

"No. I think I'll make that my little secret. He's twitchy about these things."

"He's twitchy about a lot of things," Kate smiled.

"You'll have to tell me all about that sometime."

"I've got him," Jonas said as he came back into the room. Burke trailed behind him, head down, tail limp. "But he's definitely mopey."

"I can see that," Kate said as she knelt in front of Burke. "What's wrong, fella?"

Burke glanced up at her and then quickly down again.

"It's the pot roast, isn't it? It was that bad?" Kate asked.

Burke chuffed low, barely audible.

"Well, we can rule out the pot roast," Jonas said. "Maybe he's just not feeling well."

"We'll take care of him," Kate said as she rubbed Burke's neck. "You just worry about your plan. We'll be fine."

"Right," Jonas said. Burke's demeanor made him uneasy.

"See you soon," Kate kissed Jonas's cheek, refusing to make it seem like a goodbye kiss, and then headed for the door.

Greta patted him on the shoulder. "Keep your eyes open and your mind alert, lad. Things aren't always what they seem on the surface."

Greta nodded at Raiden, holding his gaze for a moment and then she went out the door. Burke followed her and as he reached the doorway, he looked back at Jonas briefly before hanging his head again and following Kate and Greta out to the car.

"Just doggy jitters," Raiden said. "He'll be fine."

Jonas watched as the car disappeared from sight in the growing twilight before closing the door. "I hope so."

"Stop being so dour," Raiden said as he shoved a glass of whiskey into Jonas's hand. "You're supposed to be besotted with lust for my body, remember?"

"Right," Jonas downed the glass. "I'm a terrible actor. This will never work. I have no idea what I was thinking."

"I'm wounded," Raiden said.

"Don't make me kick your ass."

"Well, if you like it rough, you just have to ask," Raiden winked.

"You aren't as cute as you think you are," Jonas sighed. "But since you're the only one with any experience in this sort of thing around here, lead on, oh-wise-one."

"Glad you saw the light," Raiden said as he grabbed Jonas's arm and dragged him out to the garden. "Though it isn't much different than being with a woman, really. Simple mechanics. It's the partner that makes the difference."

"We're just acting. I don't want to know about mechanics."

"Such a prude." Raiden made a *tsk*ing noise.

"I took classes to get this prude. I have a degree in Prudology."

"Didn't go for the doctorate?" Raiden asked as he climbed the stairs of the gazebo, hauling Jonas behind him as he lit the candles, surrounding them in a soft amber glow.

"I wasn't that motivated."

"Good thing," Raiden said as he stopped in the center of the small structure and turned toward Jonas. "There may still be hope for you."

Jonas was just about to ask which side they should sit on to make the best of the charade when Raiden's mouth descended on his.

🍁 🍁 🍁

"There's a car pulling out of the drive," Liv said.

"It's her. She's got the dog and the housekeeper, but Jonas isn't with her," Reamun said. "I'll drop you off here. Go scout out the house and see if everything is alright. Seth must be around here somewhere. I'll follow the women."

Liv nodded, climbing out of the car. She was glad to be away from Reamun. As he pulled away from the curb, Liv headed through the trees lining the property, her mind alert for any sign of Seth. She didn't think he would hurt her unless provoked, but she couldn't be sure. If he saw her as any kind of threat, he would kill her without hesitation.

His power had grown stronger than her own. Like Reamun, he had given himself over fully to the deity that dwelt within him. She counted herself lucky that Nephthys was content to share her body equally until the battle was over and she was restored to her place.

Seth would not have given Horace the choice or the time. As soon as her brother had reached puberty, Seth had burst forth and Horace never even attempted to stay him. Not that he could have held Seth off for long. It would take an amazing amount of self mastery to accomplish such a task and that was a virtue her brother had never possessed.

Jonas Uhrig, on the other hand, appeared to have Horus well in hand. No one had expected him to hold out this long. She knew that Horus must be raging inside him, battling to tear himself loose, but Uhrig seemed unaffected by it.

As she made her way through the rapidly deepening gloom, she wondered if Jonas was making the wisest choice. Reamun thought him a fool. Liv wasn't so sure. Horus possessed more power and ferocity in battle than Uhrig could ever hope to achieve, but too much broiling emotion clouded Horus's mind. In such a state, he was easily fooled and prone to making rash decisions. Jonas's clear state of mind and new perspective might keep him alive.

Liv slowed as she saw the candle light ahead. She wound her way silently through the trees until she was almost even with them. She slipped behind a nearby tree and peered at the gazebo. As she watched, the light seemed to grow in intensity. The entire structure seemed aglow in a brilliant light. The latticework cascaded gracefully into the surrounding columns and the columns into the steepled roof and underlying floor forming a protective shell around two dark figures. Though the structure itself was radiant, shadows obscured the inner sanctum. The graceful silhouettes seemed intertwined in a fluid embrace, melding into one another. She leaned against the tree, her breath caught in her chest at the beauty of the vision before her.

※ ※ ※

Kate hummed the tune of 'Don't Worry, Be Happy' as she drove in an attempt to lighten Burke's mood. He sat on the floor of the passenger seat, his head resting on his paws though he wasn't asleep. He seemed unmoved by her vocal talents. Greta sat in the back seat. Glancing in the rear view mirror, Kate saw that her eyes were closed. Kate fervently wished she could nap through this and wake up to find everything was okay, but she wasn't about to delve into that degree of optimism. Not while Burke was in such a dour mood.

"What's with you, mutt? If something's wrong with Jonas's plan, you had better speak up. I need to know so I can get back there and save his butt."

Burke whimpered, burying his eyes under one furry paw.

"Come on, Burke. Tell me what's up. I feel all left out of the loop. I don't know what Jonas's plan is and I don't know why you're so gloomy. The way I see it, they have to be connected."

Burke remained silent, hiding behind the paw.

"Stop quivering like a coward and tell me what's happening!" Kate shouted. She blinked, not quite believing she had just said that. Checking the rearview mirror, she saw that her outburst didn't seem to have disturbed Greta's nap. She glanced at Burke, ready to apologize and saw that he was now sitting up, looking straight at her. His face was full of guilt and she sensed he was torn about what to do.

"I didn't mean to yell, Burke. I'm sorry. I just need to know what's going on so I can figure out what to do. We have to help Jonas in any way we can. He would do that for us."

Burke chuffed softly in agreement.

"Good. Now, is he in trouble?"

ChuffWhine.

"You don't know if he's in trouble?"

Chuff.

"But there's danger?"

Chuff.

"Something wrong with his plan?"

ChuffWhine.

"Maybe not the plan itself? Raiden?"

Chuff.

"Something is going to happen to Raiden?"

Whine.

"Is something wrong with Raiden?"

Chuff.

Kate paused, studying the road ahead as she made the last turn that would take her back to the north end of the property. Her mind was turning over possibilities, but none of them seemed to fit. Burke seemed agitated now and she knew she wouldn't figure it out in time on her own. Finally, she pulled to the side of the dirt road to park the car. Closing her eyes, she reached into herself and did what she had never done before. She let Hathor free.

❦ ❦ ❦

Reamun cut the headlights as he turned onto the private drive that ran along the north edge of the Uhrig property. He wondered why she had left just to circle back. Something wasn't right. He saw her car up ahead pulled to the side of the road. The lights were still on, and she didn't appear to be moving.

He pulled over as well, hoping that the darkness concealed his vehicle. He tried to reach her with his mind, meeting that same dead emptiness that he had before. He kept trying to push past the emptiness into her mind to see what was going on. He was about to give up when his mind was suddenly filled with a force so powerful it nearly took his breath. It was Hathor, and she wasn't happy.

Ahead, he saw her burst from the car, pausing only a moment to glare at him with fierce eyes that reminded him of a panther and bid him stay back. She moved so quickly into the trees then that she seemed to fly, the dog running quickly after her.

He sat a moment, unsure what to do. She had blocked him out again. He would try to seek out Thoth, but he was loathe to distract him while he was in the aid of Hathor. He sought out Nephthys instead. Her mind opened at once to him and he saw that she was held enraptured by something she saw. She was almost in a trance-like state and he tried calling out to her, but she could not hear him. He tried to look into her mind to see what it was she saw, but the vision was just a blur of light.

The housekeeper got out of the backseat and got behind the wheel of the car ahead. Reamun didn't particularly feel like a chat. He didn't want her to see him and become suspicious. It might prompt her to do something foolish.

He put the car in reverse and backed out the way he had come, switching on the headlights and flying back down the road toward the main entrance to the property. From here, it was nearly half a mile to the main house. If he hurried, he would beat Hathor and figure out what was going on before she came to any harm.

CHAPTER 22

Jonas was shocked, unable to move as Raiden's hands went around his waist and pulled him closer. He felt the hard press of Raiden's body against his own. *They were only supposed to be acting.* Jonas's thoughts clouded, he was unable to reconcile the fact that Raiden was kissing him with the sudden surge of heat he felt ripple through his body.

Distantly, he heard the voice of Horus within him cry out. He couldn't distinguish whether it was a cry of pain, rage, fear, lust, or some mixture of emotions. He couldn't seem to find the will to care. Jonas's hands pressed against the muscles in Raiden's chest. He meant to push him away. To get some air and much needed distance between them so he could order his thoughts. But then Raiden's hand was on his back, pulling him closer as his other hand threaded through Jonas's hair, bringing his mouth more firmly to his own.

He felt hot, dizzy, unable to focus or to find the strength to pull himself out of the embrace. His hands clenched into fists, gripping Raiden's shirt. He alternately wanted to get away and have more. He had never experienced anything as overwhelming as this.

His mind and body seemed to war with each other even as the god inside him seemed to react with longing to what was taking place. Horus said something, and this time he heard part of the god's words and his blood ran cold. *Seth.* He pushed against Raiden as hard as he could, breaking the contact between them.

Raiden caught himself on the bench, springing back up with lithe grace as Jonas backed away. Raiden pursued him slowly, his eyes glittering in the inky blackness. Jonas looked around madly, trying to decide the best course of action.

"You liked it. Admit it, Jonas."

"Seth is near…"

"You worry too much. You said yourself earlier there is still time before the final battle."

Jonas turned, but before he could move, Raiden was upon him, wrapping his arms tightly around Jonas, preventing him the use of his own arms. Jonas felt Raiden's lips on his neck and the heat was back in a sudden wave. He felt himself harden and nearly wept. He tried to stay in control of his mind, but found it impossible. Something else overwhelmed him. He was no longer in control of his own body, Horus was. The entire situation was so fundamentally weird that Jonas couldn't seem to wrap his mind around what was happening.

He felt Raiden undo the fastenings on his jeans, but he couldn't move to stop him, couldn't voice the protest in his mind. He felt as if Horus had him gagged and bound. He wondered how the god had gotten past all of his defenses. Perhaps he had been drugged. The whiskey, he thought. It would explain his inability to gain control of himself and his muddled thoughts. It would also explain the strange glow that seemed to surround the gazebo. He must have been given a hallucinogenic.

Horus wanted this, craved it, but Jonas also felt a wealth of anger and sorrow roiling through him. He was full of conflicting emotions, ones with such power and intensity that they blocked out nearly everything else. There was no clear thought involved here, and Jonas struggled to understand.

Raiden's hand closed over Jonas's erection, moving slowly in an undulant rhythm. Jonas let out a strangled cry of both pleasure and torture, wordless and weak. He knew that no one would hear it. Jonas's body fully betrayed him, he slumped back against Raiden's chest. It was useless.

"That's it," Raiden said. "Give in."

Raiden pushed him to the ground, Jonas's cheek pressed into the hard wooden bench, his knees on the floor as Raiden's weight pushed against his back. He felt the kiss of the cool night air against his flesh as Raiden divested him of his jeans. Hands ran over the newly exposed flesh, burning as they went. And then Raiden's hand curled once more around him, the weight lifted from his back.

The sensations were familiar and yet alien, yearned for and despised. Raiden leaned down and placed a kiss upon his lips and Jonas felt the press of Raiden's own arousal against his exposed skin. Once more he tried to struggle. Once more he failed.

Jonas could no longer fight, so he gave in to his body, to Horus, letting his mind drift.

🍁   🍁   🍁

Hathor flew through the night, bounding over fallen trees and over the forest terrain with the ease of a leopard. The cool wind whipped about her as she ran, the stars above gleaming brightly in the darkest of night skies. She drew on the power of the beast to give her speed and strength. She could feel Jonas's pain in her chest and she growled low in her throat as she crossed through a wide field, Burke panting madly in his effort to keep up.

She now locked Kate away deep inside, knowing the woman could do nothing to help. She felt many presences in the dark night. Nephthys was near, bound by some strange spell, Re was even now trying to outrun her. *Fool.*

Jonas had allowed Horus to slip from the confines of his soul, burning with rage and pain and what she knew was longing. Horus was also a fool, but a fool she understood. A fool with a heart that betrayed him. Thoth, ever loyal and true was behind her. And then there was Seth. He was little more than a shadow in her mind, teeming with dark frenzied emotions. She shielded herself from him. Even though his own thoughts fully occupied him, she didn't want him to see her coming.

There was an illusive whisper in the wind, urging her onward. She wasn't sure where it came from, but she heeded it.

Kate had nurtured and empowered her all these years that she slept inside of her. Like bringing an unborn babe to full maturity, she had grown strong and healthy inside the shelter of Kate's body. Now she must use all that power and skill to save not only the spirit of Horus, but also that of Jonas. She owed much to Kate and saving her beloved, who had himself sheltered and protected Horus these many years, was the way in which she would repay her debt.

She saw the glow in the distance. She knew what it was and her heart ached at the sight. Someone had drawn out the light of the Eye of Horus as a shield. Only one could do such a thing. Only Seth.

✤ ✤ ✤

Liv felt a looming presence moving rapidly toward her. At once, she knew it was Hathor. The fury of the goddess broke her out of her trance. She shivered, wondering if it were Hathor or the beast Sakhmet that would emerge from the darkness into the light.

And then she looked to the gazebo, her vision now clear, and she saw that this was not an act of pure love and devotion but one of savagery, dark emotion, and pain.

She stood, trying to move closer, but the light pushed her back. She was no match for the power that surrounded the three souls warring within. She called out in her mind to Re and she felt him close now. He was coming.

Liv looked once more to the light, knowing the torment that had brought about this achingly violent tableau. It was good that she couldn't get to them, she thought. She had no idea what she would do if she had to face the stark reality of what lay within the light.

❦   ❦   ❦

Jonas was drifting, his body given over to other forces. He ignored the voice of Horus. The wounds of the god were too much to bear. He hid instead in the dark realms of his own mind, attempting not to think, not to feel, to forget everything. All seemed so hopeless to him now. How could he hope to win against such forces? For all his basic knowledge of mythology and history and the general situation, he had no power to stop what was happening. He was almost completely lost when a feminine voice, trembling with rage, filled his mind.

Fight him, it said

I can't.

You can. Fight him, Jonas.

Lost.

No! I am coming, but you must fight him. Do not let Seth take this power over you for it cannot be undone if he finishes the deed.

Seth? Jonas distantly remembered the cry of Horus.

Yes, Jonas. He is not your friend. He never was. He is Seth and he is trying to steal your power and the power of Horus. Horus cannot see this, for he is in turmoil.

I will fight, Jonas tried to cling to his tenuous resolve.

Suddenly coming back to his body, feeling the sensations fully, he was nearly overwhelmed once again. He drew on the resolve deep within himself that he had used to control Horus all these years and broke free of the spell of lethargy and submission that had overcome him. The light surrounding them seemed to fade and he felt Seth's hand clamp on his shoulder.

"You cannot win, Jonas," he hissed, thrusting into Jonas's body with increasing violence. It was the same voice he had heard the night Seth had murdered Millie.

Seth's hand tightened painfully around Jonas's flagging erection. Jonas concentrated on the pain, making it easier to forget the will of Horus.

"I won't let you do this." Jonas gritted his teeth and pushed back against Seth.

It wasn't enough to loose the other from his body, but it was enough to give him pause. Jonas was still weak, but he was determined to stop Seth before it was too late. He pushed again, but Seth was unyielding, tightening his hold on Jonas.

Still battling the demands of his body, Jonas prepared to push back once more, bracing his arms against the bench when the fierce cry of a wildcat split through the night. Seth froze, knowing the sound of the cry that heralded the ancient goddess of war. Jonas knew this was his only chance. He pushed back with all his strength, coming forward again as quickly as he could, effectively separating himself from Seth. He fell to the floor, lying on his back, heaving with the effort.

The incandescent light surrounding them had gone out, leaving only the glow of the candles. Seth moved to reach for him, but a black panther, graceful and deadly sprang from the night to plant itself between them. It bared its teeth, growling low as Seth pulled back his hand. Then another figure emerged from behind Jonas. It was the dog, also baring its teeth, a warning growl issuing from its throat.

"You win the battle," Seth said. "But not the war."

Seth rolled, planting his feet on the ground and fled so swiftly into the night that he seemed to disappear.

Jonas relaxed back onto the floor of the gazebo, all his strength gone. Burke nuzzled his neck, whimpering.

"S'okay, boy," Jonas whispered. "Where'd you find your friend?"

"That," came a deep voice from the steps, "is my beloved and much feared daughter. In her somewhere is your Kate. I believe. I can't be certain that she didn't eat her for a snack." The sarcasm was evident in the voice.

Jonas heard the panther growl again, but this time it wasn't one that threatened a deadly attack.

"A family reunion," Jonas said as his eyes closed. "How nice."

The world went black.

CHAPTER 23

❈

Warmth surrounded Jonas, seeping into his muscles, chasing away the pain. He felt a cloth glide across his skin, and he flinched, opening his eyes.

"Shh. It's okay, lad," Greta said.

Jonas focused on her face, "Where's Kate?" Jonas tried to sit up, but pain shot up his spine.

"No moving," Greta said. "Bad idea."

"I figured that out, thanks. Kate?"

"She's sleeping. Surprisingly, Sakhmet gave her the body back. No beer required."

"Burke?" Jonas asked.

"He's feeling guilty and wretched and basically despondent, but he'll come around. I told him to keep an eye on Kate to give him something to do."

"Thank you, Greta. You know everything that's happening, don't you?"

"Of course I do," she said. "Who else would keep you from getting yourself killed if not for me?"

"Uncle Henry told you about what happened? About the research he did after?"

"He told me what he found. He knew you would need help some day and that Millie might not be there to give it."

"There was a man in the garden. Do you know who he is?"

"Reamun," she said. "Re, Ra, Raymond. He's not a very mannerly person. He likes things his way."

"You don't like him?" Jonas was tired, but trying to follow what she was telling him.

"He's not evil. He can even be a benevolent god. Unless his own fate is on the line. Then things get ugly."

"How ugly?" Jonas asked.

"Isn't the current situation ugly enough for you?"

"He's responsible for this?"

"A great deal of it. He tried to separate Horus and Seth with the help of Isis and others. It didn't go so well."

"I'll say," Jonas said.

"Seth and Horus were both miserable after they were parted. They were angry and torn and enraged beyond measure. At each other, at everyone else, at the whole world. Seth never murdered Osiris. He helped him die. It was something that had to be to preserve the balance, and Osiris knew this. But they used it to turn Horus against him. To instill doubt and mistrust. Eventually they were able to use the lie to tear Seth and Horus apart. When chaos would have taken over, Re put us all to sleep to wait for another day when Horus and Seth would battle it out to the death and one would emerge victorious. And when we awoke inside the bodies of our human companions, he began his little game. Setting Horus and Seth against each other."

"You said *us*."

"Did I?" Greta asked.

"Yes, you did. You were there, weren't you? At the dig site. You were inside."

Greta smiled. "You always were a smart boy. Neither Henry nor Millie ever suspected. I had gone with them, of course. Millie always needed people to do things for her. She barely noticed me. Servants are invisible to most people. It was easy for me to sneak inside after them and keep to the shadows. I was curious."

"But didn't you get taken to the hospital with the rest of them?"

"No. I never lost consciousness. I sat in the shadows and waited while they took the others out. I snuck out just as I had snuck in. I was afraid they would blame me for what happened. No one notices servants until something goes wrong. Then we get the blame."

"Why didn't you lose consciousness? Why can none of us sense who you are?"

"Because the one who took me was unlike the others. He was neither living nor dead," Greta said.

"He who?"

"You know the answer to that," she said.

Jonas realized he did. He thought about what she said about the battle constructed by Re to decide the victor. "What if no one wins?"

"Someone has to win," she said.

"But what if no one does? What happens if it's a draw?"

Her hand stopped and she stared down at him. Her eyes held keen interest. "How?"

"You tell me."

She thought for a moment, seeming to hesitate. "There is only one way Seth and Horus will ever be at peace," she said.

"And what is that one way?"

"Are you sure you want to know? After what happened, I would think you would want to just kill him and be done with it."

"I want to do what is right," Jonas said.

He had at first wondered how he had not seen Seth in Raiden before, but he knew the truth. He hadn't wanted to see it. He hadn't been ready. And now that he knew, he couldn't merely kill him and be done with it. No matter what had been inflicted upon him, Jonas knew that there was good in him. There was still a light, one that shone brightly, deep within Seth's tortured soul.

If he hadn't come to know him so well through Raiden, he would never have seen the possibility of redemption. He would simply have continued to think of him as a two-dimensional monster that leapt out of a nightmare.

"I believe you already know what needs to be done," Greta said. "To undo the pain of the past, you must heal the wound."

"Rejoin them," Jonas said. "But how?"

CHAPTER 24

❀

Kate woke late in the afternoon, feeling as if she could sleep another six hours. Light filtered in through gossamer curtains, filling the room with a warming glow. She rolled over in bed and saw that Jonas was sitting up, his back against the headboard, staring at the ceiling.

"Jonas?"

"Hmm?"

"Are you alright?"

"Yes. You?"

"I'm fine, but last night you…"

"I know. It's okay. Everything is going to work out," Jonas said, his eyes still fixed on the ceiling.

She sat up, noting that the bruises that had covered him the night before were almost gone now. She wanted to reach out and touch him, but she was also afraid that he wasn't ready for it.

"Where's Burke?" she asked.

"Downstairs with Greta keeping an eye on Re and Liv."

"Liv? Isn't she the one who Rob left the party with?"

"Yes."

"And she's here? In the house?"

"Yes."

"You trust her?"

"More than I trust Re, but that isn't saying a lot. The part of her that is human is fairly honest. She still cares about the value of life and the outcome of this thing. The part of her that is not cares only about the outcome."

"You're going to see him, aren't you? Seth."

"I have to. I have to end this. It's time."

"Can't you give it a few days? What he did to you last night was…"

"It was anger and pain. Nothing more."

"How can you say that?"

"It's the truth. I felt no more tortured than he did."

"How do you know this?"

"I can feel it. His emotions. I can see the memories."

"What are you going to do?"

"I'm going to fix it. Everything they destroyed. Everything the other gods tore apart because of their selfishness and their vanity. They won't like it. You'll have to make sure they don't interfere. Greta will help you."

"Okay," she said. She studied his face. "You aren't going to kill him." It wasn't a question.

"No," Jonas confirmed. "I'm not."

"Why?"

"Because it would fix nothing. It would merely give rise to a new set of problems."

It suddenly dawned on her that he was planning to rejoin the two gods. "You're going to do it? Even after what he did to you?"

"What he did to me isn't an issue."

"It is to me," she said.

"It isn't about me, Kate. It's about right and wrong. Good versus evil. Few things in life are so clear cut."

"I think you're in denial," she said.

"Maybe. Maybe I have to be. Come on, there's a lot to do."

🍁   🍁   🍁

When Kate and Jonas went downstairs, they found Reamun and Liv talking in low voices over the kitchen table. Greta was preparing dinner while Burke sat nearby, and though he looked as if he were gazing out the back window, Jonas knew he was listening to their conversation. People rarely paid attention to animals and servants, even when those animals and servants were gods.

"Made yourselves comfortable?" Jonas asked.

The two looked up simultaneously to smile and nod. Jonas noted that Reamun was about five foot nine and had the build of a runner. He looked no more threatening in daylight than a rat, but inside that façade was the diabolical mind of an ancient god.

"You are going to kill him tonight?" Reamun asked.

"It will be taken care of," Jonas said dismissively. He went to start a pot of coffee.

"How? How will you do this?" Reamun was insistent.

"You needn't concern yourself," Jonas said. "I have it in hand."

Reamun laughed. "As you had it in hand last night?"

"Shut up, Re," Liv warned.

Kate wanted to strangle the man. Burke merely growled. Greta continued chopping vegetables. Jonas continued making coffee.

"It is not only the fate of yourself and Horus at stake," Reamun continued.

"I'm well aware."

"I will come with you."

"No," Jonas said. "You will stay here with the others. Burke is coming with me. No one will interfere. The plan will work."

Reamun burst out of his chair and crossed to stand directly in front of Jonas, seething with frustration. "You are no more than a mortal man. You cannot hope to win without my guidance!"

Jonas shoved him back against the wall before he had any chance to react and closed his hand around the other man's throat as he lifted him off the floor. "I could kill you now. You are no more immortal than I am in that body you possess. Stay out of my way, little man."

Reamun sputtered in his anger, his face turning red as he tried to breathe. "You cannot speak to me this way," he managed to squeak.

"Oh?" Jonas let go, and Reamun dropped to the floor, gasping for air.

"We should take him to the coat room and lock it from the outside," Greta said.

"There's a lock on the outside?" Kate asked.

"Yes. Henry liked to drink, but Millie didn't like his penchant for breaking things when he did. That was their compromise."

Jonas smiled and shook his head. He looked down at Reamun who was still coughing and wheezing. Leaning down, he hefted the man over his shoulder and headed down the hall. Kate went ahead of him and opened the door while Liv and Burke followed. Greta remained in the kitchen.

The room was about sixteen feet square with a polished marble floor. The back wall was fitted with racks on which several coats hung. The other two walls held large mirrors with velvet covered chaise lounges beneath. A plush rug with an intricately woven Chinese dragon lay in the center of the floor. When Jonas dumped Reamun on the rug, Liv looked up at him.

"Maybe you should lock me in here as well," she said.

"You sure?" Jonas asked.

She nodded. "I know what you're going to do. I think it's good, but Nephthys might not see it that way. Maybe once you're gone Kate can watch us in the study or something. Nep and Re will know enough not to cross her if she has the gun. Besides, she's got fangs when she's angry," Liv grinned.

"That she does," Jonas smiled.

"It's a pain in the ass to keep them clean," Kate said. "You should try flossing fangs."

Chuff, Burke said.

"At least someone understands your plight," Jonas winked.

"You can't...do this," Reamun said from the floor.

"Practically already done," Jonas said. "Just sit back and enjoy your stay in the coat room."

"I made something for you," Liv said. "It's in the study. I thought it might be useful."

"Thank you," Jonas said. "If you need anything, just shout."

With a last nod at Liv, Jonas, Burke, and Kate left the room, locking it behind them.

"Wonder what she left you," Kate said.

"Let's go find out."

Jonas opened the door to the study, Burke and Kate followed him in. Lying on the desk was a black robe. Jonas lifted it, running his finger over the golden threads that shimmered on the trim hand woven into tiny hieroglyphs.

"What does it say?"

"It's the story of Horus and Seth," Jonas said. He couldn't read hieroglyphs any more than Kate could, but he knew.

"It would have taken months, maybe years to do all that."

"Yeah."

"She knew?"

"Maybe it was just a wish," Jonas said. "A hope that it would be needed."

"Are you going to wear it?"

Jonas looked at Burke.

Chuff.

"I would say that's a yes."

Kate looked at the clock on the wall and Jonas followed her eyes.

"I should get ready," he said.

"Yeah," she nodded.

He carefully folded the robe, laying it over his arm. "Want to come?"

"Shower?"
"Yeah."
She grinned. "I'm there."
"Can you hold down the fort with Greta while we're gone, pal?"
Chuff.

※   ※   ※

They took their time in the shower, neither one wanting it to end. When the water began to get chilly, they both knew it was time. They toweled each other off, the light caresses if fingers and lips lingering. When they were both dry, Kate helped Jonas slip on the robe. He kissed her one last time before taking her hand and heading down the steps.

In the study, Jonas picked up the phone and dialed the number, not daring to breathe. Kate's hand tightened around his and he squeezed back reassuringly. He heard the soft click as the connection was made, but there was only silence at the other end. He could feel him there, listening.

"I need to see you," Jonas said.

"Yes. The time has come. You know what must happen?"

"I do. However, I don't think you know."

"What foolishness is this?"

"There is a better way. A way in which we both win," Jonas said.

"Lies."

"I do not lie to you. How could I? There was a time when we could deceive each other, but no more. You can see my heart and mind just as I see yours."

There was a pause and then, "I will meet with you in the far field on the north end of the estate in ten minutes."

"I'll be there."

Jonas hung up the phone and looked at Kate. Her eyes filled with fear. "It will be alright," he said.

"You don't know that. You can't promise me that. What if this doesn't work?"

"It will work. It has to."

"But if you're wrong…"

"Then all the world is no worse off than it would be otherwise," Jonas said.

"But you'll be dead," Kate whispered. "I couldn't bear that, Jonas."

He cupped her cheek, bending to brush his lips across her forehead. "Trust in me."

She drew in a shaky breath and nodded. "I'll see that Re and Liv stay put and don't interfere."

Jonas kissed her lips one last time before turning and heading out the door, Burke close behind.

CHAPTER 25

The two ran through the night to the northern field as quickly as they could. Seth would no doubt already be waiting. Jonas felt the presence inside him try to force its way to the surface, but he once again quelled it, tightening his inner-hold. He must hold out just a little while longer.

The night was cold, the dark sky clear and shimmering with thousands of stars. He could hear his heart pounding in his ears. His scalp seemed to tighten and prickle with tiny pinpoints of electricity.

Jonas reached the field, and as he had thought, Seth was waiting there. He was no longer Raiden, nor was he Horace Sampson. Jonas stopped and stood staring at Seth, feeling the energy that vibrated within him.

Memories flashed through his mind. Memories of another time, another place, long ago when the world of man was young and gods ruled with stern dominion. The shadowed landscape around them seemed to morph before his eyes. Where there was once a leaf laden ground and trees, there was now golden sand shimmering beneath his feet. The moon shone clearly in a star filled sky. Jonas had never before seen so many stars. And then the mirage was gone, the world shifting back to the present.

"You cannot fault me my destiny," Seth said as he approached. His movements were liquid grace. His naked body gleamed in the moonlight. "Those people, those mortals had to die so that I could regain my power. I am driven to it just as you are driven to try to stop me. We are no more than pawns."

Jonas made no move to back away as the graceful god approached. He felt some voice deep within him screaming in rage and agony to be set free, to right the wrongs done by this being. Jonas closed his eyes briefly, locking away the voice, but drawing on the knowledge he found within. He opened his eyes. Seth was standing directly before him now, his face mere inches from Jonas's.

"Yet you are not he who would destroy me out of vengeance. Not fully. Not as I am Seth. Where does Horus hide?"

"He is here, within me. His very spirit calls out to slay you," Jonas said.

Seth ran the back of his hand over Jonas's cheek, and then he lowered his head to run his tongue along Jonas's collarbone. "And yet you come to me unarmed. You have him locked inside you, I feel him there. What game do you play?"

"I play no game," Jonas said. "Do you not wish to be free?"

"Free?" Seth asked. He glided a hand over Jonas's hip. "No one is ever free from the powers. We will chase each other to the end of days until one of us becomes the victor."

"There is another way," Jonas whispered. He caught Seth's hand in his own. "Join with me as we once did. Only this time we will do it right. Our powers converged into one would balance all."

"It isn't possible," Seth said.

"It *is* possible. They never gave us that choice, Seth. Because that choice meant that they would no longer be needed. They have distracted and blinded us, turning us against each other since the beginning of time. If we unite our powers in one unhindered embrace, we will both win."

Seth went still. "You would do this?"

Jonas nodded though the voice inside him raged and bellowed to be set free.

"Why?" Seth asked, his breath caressing Jonas's neck.

"Because none of us will ever be truly free until it is done. No matter which of us won the battle, we would still be the pawns of another. As will all the creatures of Earth. Think of it, Seth."

"You forget the maiming done unto me. For all to be made balanced, our life-giving seed must flow together as one. The unity can be completed no other way. This thing you ask cannot be done," Seth said.

"As once the Eye of Horus was grievously injured and then restored, so will I see your body restored to its full glory."

Burke appeared then, emerging from the trees to stand before Seth. As he approached, he took the form of a young man. Brown skin, shoulder-length ebony hair weaved into tiny braids, his only raiment was an intricately woven loincloth, shot through with threads of gold, red, yellow, and pearl. His semblance was humble, though his eyes held great wisdom.

Dark eyes shimmering, Seth kneeled before him. "Djeheuty," he whispered. "My son. Long has it been since I looked into your eyes."

"Father," the young and yet ancient man said, gathering Seth's hands in his own, pressing them to his chest as he bowed his head.

"Lie down, and you will be made whole again," Jonas said.

Seth looked to Djeheuty, who nodded in reassurance. "This mortal speaks the truth. Though he is not the voice of Horus, he carries in him my father's soul. Though the great god would deny his own true wisdom, his heart beckons for this. I have felt it."

"Then it shall be so." Taking a deep breath, Seth lowered his tall form to the ground, spreading out on the grass. He closed his eyes, and chanted softly as Djeheuty approached, chanting a spell of his own as he knelt beside the prone form of his father.

Jonas watched with awe as a light seemed to emanate from Seth's body. The young man at his side ran lightly caressing fingertips over Seth as he spoke ancient words of restoration and magic. Jonas felt a surge of rage wash through him as Horus struggled to break free of his confines and emerge to stop this healing. Jonas forced him back down, though he wasn't sure how long he could keep him chained.

Djeheuty sensed the war going on within Jonas, and though he felt deeply for the father trapped within, he knew this was the only way to bring peace. He worked quickly, Seth's body nearly rising from the ground with the power of the magic that set fire to his blood.

And then it was done, Seth lay limp on the ground, his breath coming in great gasps. Djeheuty stood, nodding to Jonas that it was done before taking his leave. Jonas approached the still form of Seth. Though his energy waned from the healing, his eyes were open and he looked upon Jonas with a mixture of fear and longing.

Jonas untied the sash of his robe, the black silk parting and revealing his long finely muscled form. He shrugged his shoulders, letting the robe fall to the ground.

Seth's eyes followed him intently, though he made no move. He watched as Jonas knelt between his thighs, felt his warm hands as they trailed over his belly. For the first time in millennia, he felt his body react with a powerful surge. He sucked in a breath as Jonas placed his lips just below his navel.

Jonas closed his eyes, letting his mind drift freely while still restraining Horus with all his will. With hands, tongue, and lips, he made himself more familiar with Seth's body. Each taste and touch recalled a memory from the past. Soon he too was lost in the moment.

Ancient images and sensations filled his mind and body from a time long ago when these two souls had joined in loving embrace. The raging voice within him seemed farther away now and his previous fear that he would be incapable of rousing himself to the level of ardor the situation demanded had long fled from his mind.

"Please," Seth said in a strangled moan. His plea was both honest and breathtaking. Here before him lay one of the most powerful gods of ancient times, and only Jonas could fill his need.

Jonas felt Seth's muscles tense, and he gazed into Jonas's eyes for a long time. Eternities seemed to pass as he spoke silent words into Jonas's soul and the soul of the one who dwelt within, still struggling against his fate.

Jonas then raised himself onto his knees, his eyes remaining locked with Seth's emerald stare as he lifted first one leg and then the other over his shoulders to allow him access. Seth reached forward, guiding Jonas into him.

With one swift thrust, Jonas was sheathed within the body of the ancient god, and a cry of both ecstasy and pain left his lips, though the voice was not his own. Horus had finally broken free of his bonds, but too late. He too was locked within the passion and sensual pull of the moment, and he thrust into Seth again and again, seeking the release that could only be found within this other god. His enemy, his lover, his kindred. Most hated and beloved of all he had ever known.

Seth was instantly aware of the other now. He felt his body tighten, the ache of thousands of years finally being soothed as his lover drove deeply within him, their bodies now one.

The heavens crashed with lightning and thunder as both roared with their release, their seed intertwining, creating a bond that was more powerful than any spell or incantation to ever have been uttered in the history of Earth. In that moment, Horus and Seth melded into one eternal being.

✤   ✤   ✤

Kate nearly jumped out of her chair when the lightning and thunder crashed overhead. Greta didn't so much as pause in the rhythmic movements she made as she knitted a white doily. Kate kept the gun trained on Reamun as she glanced out the window. Liv sat nearby, but showed no signs of any emotion as she stared at the wall. When she looked back, Reamun was slumped in his seat, his eyes staring but unseeing. His entire countenance showing defeat.

"It is over," he said. His voice seemed devoid of its earlier baritone, his eyes empty, as if he were now only an empty shell.

Relief swept through her. Jonas had been successful, but at what price? Her stomach tightened as she wondered what would become of him after this joining. There was a yelp and then a scratching at the front door and Kate rushed out into the foyer, pulling it open.

On the porch Jonas lay naked, his eyes closed. He was utterly still, his skin deathly pale and softly glowing in the moonlight. She rushed forward and knelt beside him.

"Jonas!" She checked for a pulse, but found none. "No!" she screamed. She looked at Burke. "Save him, damnit!"

Burke looked at her helplessly and whimpered.

"No," she whispered, gathering Jonas's head into her lap. "Please, Jonas. Please." His skin was frighteningly cold. She smoothed his hair back from his face. "Live, damn you!" she sobbed.

"Give him to me," Greta said softly from behind Kate.

She knelt and scooped Jonas in her arms and carried him inside as if he weighed no more than a feather. Kate stared in amazement as Greta went into the house. Burke nudged her shoulder. Coming back to her senses, she followed Greta inside.

Greta had laid Jonas down on the couch in the drawing room. Now she stood over him, her hands gliding just above his body as she spoke quickly in a forgotten language. Kate wanted to ask a thousand questions, but she remained silent, staring as Greta continued the ritual.

Suddenly Jonas coughed, his body wracked with shivers which led to an even more violent fit of coughing. Kate scrambled forward as Greta stepped back to allow her to pass. Kate lifted him to a sitting position, leaning his tall frame against her as she wept now with relief and murmured soothing words, rubbing his back.

Jonas curled into her, feeling a cold that went deep within his soul. There was no sense of the other within him any longer. He remembered nothing after that first encompassing thrust. The rest was darkness.

Burke padded into the room with a blanket clenched between his teeth and trailing behind him. Kate wrapped it around both Jonas and herself, her arms going about his shoulders as he clung to her, still shaking.

"Kate," Jonas managed to say.

"I'm here, Jonas. Don't try to talk just yet," Kate said, her arms tightening around him.

"Need you."

"I know," she said. She looked up to as Greta what had happened, but the woman was gone.

CHAPTER 26

When Jonas woke again, he was in a large soft bed under several layers of blankets. Kate was curled up next to him. Though he didn't remember taking a bath, his hair was still slightly damp. He couldn't imagine that Kate had been able to drag him to the bathtub herself.

Though he still felt very cold, the warmth of her body against his seemed to chase away most of the chill. He closed his eyes, trying to feel the presence within him, but found nothing. Horus was gone.

He smoothed a hand over Kate's hair. She stirred slightly and looked up at him with a smile.

"Feeling better?" she asked.

"Much."

"Horus?"

"Gone," he said.

"So is Hathor."

"What about Reamun and Liv?"

"I don't know. When I went back inside they were gone. No sign of them. Their car was gone as well."

"Horace Sampson?"

"I think he died a long time ago, giving his body over to Seth, but I haven't seen him. Wherever Seth is, he and Horus are bound together."

"What about Burke?" Jonas asked.

"He's still the same old Burke. Hard to tell."

"My enigmatic dog," Jonas smiled. "I guess Greta is gone as well?"

Kate nodded. "She disappeared right after she brought you back. I was going to ask her how she did it, but she was gone."

"Osiris," Jonas said. "Greta was at the dig site when it happened. No one ever knew. Until she told me last night. Osiris wanted to right all the wrongs that he willingly died to prevent in the first place. He was just waiting for the right time."

"Greta told you how to do it?"

Jonas nodded. "Osiris had the benefit of knowing the full truth of what happened, of being separated from the other gods by his death and rebirth. He was unlike them enough to be able to see things clearly and alike enough to come up with a plan that would restore balance."

"But Osiris was still within Greta after you completed the reunification of Horus and Seth. He didn't get taken away like the rest of them."

"No," Jonas said. "I imagine he's different enough to have been spared their fate."

"I wonder what he'll do. Since he wasn't set free, is he trapped in her body?"

"I don't know. I think he probably had a way out of that as well. I get the feeling he had this planned for a very long time."

"Most likely. It's still disturbing to think of a god roaming the earth."

"At least there aren't as many as there were. One seems much more reasonable."

"So what do we do now that the world is safe?"

"Get married. Buy a nice little house somewhere. Have a couple kids," Jonas said. "Nice big yard for Burke."

"I always wanted to live in a row house."

"You did not."

"Okay, maybe not always. Just since I saw yours. Needs some sprucing up though," she said.

"So you're marrying me for my house?"

"Not just the house."

"No?"

"Nope. It's mostly the dog."

Author's Note

There is much about ancient Egypt that we do not know. The assertion herein that modern Egyptology is blind to the facts is something that becomes more painfully obvious as academia repeatedly denounces clear evidence that our current thinking about that civilization is misguided. While this book is entirely fiction, I have done my best to base it on factual evidence, some of which I'm sure would be heartily contested by Egyptologists.

I am currently at work on my next book, Crossing the Rubicon, in which I will continue this tale. An excerpt follows on the next page.

Prologue

Snow falls steadily through the fading twilight. Like a veil of shimmering phosphorescence, it blankets the land beyond the forest. The hush of the night is full of unspoken words echoing solemnly through the trees. As if in response, the wind picks up briefly, rattling barren limbs against one another in a soft murmur of answer.

I feel now the movement of time as never before. I have seen the dawn of the first sunrise. I have spent thousands of years living in the beauty and wonder of the sheltering arms of this realm. To leave this most beloved place, even at the brink of the steady downward slope that would know only the pain and heartache of its decline, I find its pull is no less compelling for all the sorrow that had passed and lay yet ahead.

The fabric of my soul is so acutely interwoven with the threads of this world that the very thought of leaving brings me to an almost sudden and irrational fear that once I have turned my back, it will cease to exist. As if it were just as dependant upon me for sustenance and fruition as I have been upon it for millennia.

Unbidden, an image of my father comes into my mind. He was not yet my father when first we met. It was only later, after the doctors had told him that his unborn child had little hope of surviving to birth and even less of reaching the age of two that I would use my powers to preserve that most precious life. A life that became my own.

I am as much the son of Jonas and Kate Uhrig as I am an ancient. My personality, my values, my love of life all comes from my devoted parents. Yet within me lies the knowledge, the memories, and the powers of the ancient that sacrificed his autonomy so that I may live. Just as he had long ago sacrificed himself for his own son. He is me and I am him. We are one.

Though by my mere existence in the world I had cheated fate the moment I had been born and continued to cheat it every year that I continued to live showing no signs of any physical malady as the doctors had warned, no one, not even the wise ancient who gave himself over one cool October night centuries ago, could have imagined the fantastical events of my life. Even now, most of the world passes on unaware of the dark machinations and the kaleidoscope of horrors that I have known.

This blissful ignorance can no longer continue. I cannot move on beyond this realm, if in fact that is what my final decision may be, without leaving some account of what has transpired to bring us all to this place. This most grievous place.

On this precipice of indecision I wait. Soon she will come. The one who will tell the tale of my life as it must be told if there is any hope for the future. Perhaps there is some vanity in this act.

I am not immune to this basic human need to leave my mark upon the world. For I am fundamentally human. Born to this world of woman. My ancient knowledge and power a mere extension of genetic melding of human DNA that took place hundreds of years ago within Kate Uhrig's womb.

However, it is primarily for the purpose of preserving the knowledge which I have gained over the many years of my varied existence that I wish my tale to be told. The truth, or at least my perspective of the truth, may one day prove useful for those that come after. At the very least it will be a documentation of the events that have led me here.

0-595-26887-0